In praise of Carrie Alexander & Black Velvet

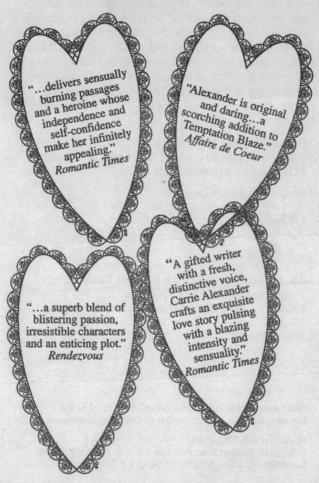

My dear readers,

This book is my valentine to you. It's as rich and sinful as a heart-shaped box of yummy imported chocolates— but with no nasty calories! So put a bottle of champagne on ice, throw a log on the fire, curl up with a loved one (dogs and cats count, too) and *indulge* yourself. After all, it's not every woman who gets to spend her Valentine's Day with the likes of Nikolas, Peter and Quinn—three devastating males who really know how to make a woman's toes curl. And who would know better than Madame X.

If you enjoy this Valentine treat as much as I think you will, send a note to my alter ego, Carrie Alexander, at P.O. Box 611, Marquette, MI 49855.

Happy Valentine's Day,

Madame X

P.S. I hope you enjoyed the first two Black Velvet Temptations, #689 *Black Velvet* and #704 *A Touch of Black Velvet*.

BLACK VELVET VALENTINES

Secrets of the Heart
Two Hearts
Heart's Desire

Carrie Alexander

HARLEQUIN®

TORONTO • NEW YORK • LONDON
AMSTERDAM • PARIS • SYDNEY • HAMBURG
STOCKHOLM • ATHENS • TOKYO • MILAN • MADRID
PRAGUE • WARSAW • BUDAPEST • AUCKLAND

ISBN 0-373-25820-8

BLACK VELVET VALENTINES

Printed in U.S.A.

BLACK VELVET
VALENTINES

Secrets of the Heart

You never know where or how love will find you. Sometimes it's through arousingly sensuous black velvet valentines...sent by a stranger.

1

THE FIRST VALENTINE came in the mail. Charlotte thought it must be a mistake.

For one thing, even though she was only twenty-five, she hadn't received a valentine from a man in several years—not since Terrence had left and her father had passed away. For another—she checked her desk calendar, unsure of the date, but, yes—Valentine's Day was still a week away. No matter. She didn't know anyone who'd send her a valentine, on time or not.

A mistake. Addressed to her. Charlotte Colfax.

Absently twining a long strand of antique pearls around her fingers, Charlotte mulled over the curious development in her usual deliberate way. The envelope was a thick, gold-and cream-colored vellum, mottled like buttermilk. There was a New York postmark. Unfamiliar handwriting. Masculine. The card inside…

With her fingertips she caressed the black velveteen flocking of the lacy hearts that decorated the front of the valentine. She brought it up to her face, rubbed it lightly against her cheek, then caught herself with a sharp exclamation of surprise.

Stupid girl. Silly girl—dreaming your life away. Twenty-two months after Esme Colfax's death, her harsh voice still echoed inside Charlotte's head.

Charlotte dropped the card without opening it and got up to pace the library, one hand rubbing at the nape of her bent neck. Suddenly the mass of her pinned-up hair seemed a burden too heavy to bear.

Her lips moved, forming the words of her silent battle. Even though she hadn't been able to entirely heal the damage Esme Colfax had done to her self-esteem, she had learned to combat the insidious seeds of doubt planted by her spiteful stepmother.

Deliberately, Charlotte repeated to herself that she was a fine person, good and kind and giving. She was productive in her small way. She caused no harm or pain. No trouble.

I am not a stupid, useless girl.

Thus fortified, Charlotte stopped pacing and returned to the desk—to the delicious distraction of the valentine. At least she hoped it was a valentine.

"Hope springs eternal," she said, smiling because feminine optimism had won out over self-doubt, and even over her lingering grief at her father's death. Apparently, a surprise valentine was the tonic she'd been needing.

A valentine, she thought. *Astonishing!*

Who could have sent it? She was almost afraid to look, leery that it would prove to be only a computer-generated token from her broker, attorney or accountant. Not likely, though; the firms she dealt with concerning the Colfax inheritance were the epitome of stodgy professionalism. But Charlotte couldn't think of anyone else, which was a sad—and appropriate—comment on her social life.

Quickly now, she picked up the valentine and looked inside.

The blood drained from her face as she read the handwritten message, then rose precipitously as she read it again, her cheeks flushing hotter and hotter until beads of perspiration popped out at her hairline.

She touched the bun anchored at the base of her skull.

Obviously a mistake, said the inner voice. Charlotte dropped the card. It wasn't meant for her.

Yet her name was on the envelope. Her Fifth Avenue, Manhattan address.

With a soft moan, she sank into her father's old leather desk chair, the chair that was usually so comforting in her loneliness. For once she didn't notice the familiar padded contours or the faint smoke-and-leather scent that usually brought back memories of evenings in the library with her father, him smoking a pipe at his desk, and her sitting before the fire, still a carefree child in the time before Esme's arrival, reading books about fairy-tale princesses and wicked stepmothers.

After all these years, the grown-up Charlotte Colfax finally had something more intriguing to read.

The valentine was unsigned, its message short and irrefutably adult. She kept staring at it, waiting for it to make sense.

I want to feel your hair sliding through my fingers like silk

A hairdresser! Charlotte thought wildly. Perhaps the card was an advertisement for a new salon.

She knew it wasn't.

I want to feel your hair

Charlotte pressed her hand against her warm brow, then slipped it over the smooth curve of her blond head and down to the heavy lump of the well-pinned bun. She touched several hairpins, making certain they were in place.

sliding through my fingers

Rarely did she let down her hair. It was so long it was cumbersome, so fine that it easily became tangled. Only on the roof of her penthouse apartment, in the wind, when she succumbed to her princess daydreams, did she sometimes let it loose. And no one could have seen her there. Then how…?

like silk

She sat back, worrying the long double rope of pearls that she always wore because they had belonged to the mother she could scarcely remember. The leather armchair creaked companionably when she pressed her shoulders against it. "All right," she whispered, trying to calm herself. "Think." She closed her eyes to concentrate, found she still couldn't and resorted to her address book. She paged through it frantically, looking for someone, anyone. One name, however far-fetched.

There was no one. Absolutely no one. Charlotte Colfax did not know a single man who could have mailed her such an astonishing valentine.

CHARLOTTE FRETTED ABOUT the whys and wherefores and what-ifs of the black velvet valentine all the next morning. She did no work at all, though usually she was diligent from 8:00 a.m. to half past noon, toiling on her dissertation concerning the life and literature of Jane Austen. For once, the present was more interesting to Charlotte than the courtship of Emma Woodhouse and Mr. Knightley.

Being a stickler for minutiae, she finally settled on what nagged at her about the anonymous valentine; it was the missing punctuation. She was perplexed, not...aroused. The line should have properly concluded with a period: *I want to feel your hair sliding through my fingers like silk.* Because there was no period, she was led to suspect that there would be a continuation in the correspondence. One could hardly expect her to settle down with her usual research tools when the morning mail was due any moment!

Charlotte smiled wryly to herself. Clearly her life contained a sorry dearth of excitement if a missing punctuation mark was all it took to set her heart fluttering like the pigeons on the rooftop parapets. She should not raise her hopes when they were sure to be disappointed. But that was Esme talking, wasn't it?

Charlotte began going through her address book again, page by page. Although the number of her personal acquaintances—particularly those of the male persuasion—had narrowed in the past few years, she managed to dredge up a few unlikely names. Terrence White for one. Their college romance had been naive, idealistic—at least on her part—and, thankfully, brief. If not for the fact that Terrence was still bumming around Europe, he could have penned the poetic valentine message. He certainly would have signed it, though, Charlotte decided. Most lavishly, at that. Terrence White was not the anonymous type.

Of the other just barely possible candidates, she had contact with only one on a regular basis. And the thought of her old college professor, Dr. Hadley Alcorn, sending her a suggestive valentine was simply…

In a word, *impossible.* Charlotte laughed hollowly, suddenly all too aware of just how alone she was. She had a few girlfriends, and there was Hattie, of course. But ever since the wrenching shock of Terrence's defection, followed by the even more devastating loss of her father, Charlotte had hidden herself away behind the thick walls of her apartment building. The Colfax Towers was an eccentric stone edifice known to New Yorkers as simply "The Castle" because of its pair of crenellated granite towers with a bird's-eye view of swank Fifth Avenue and Central Park.

Charlotte was not a true Rapunzel, however. Hers had been a self-imposed isolation. But now, finally, the black velvet valentine had given her an impetus for change. If only she could identify its source…

Casting about for another name, she thought again of the league of professional money men she'd inherited when her father and stepmother were killed in a car accident on a German autobahn. She'd forgotten that one of the lawyers was under the age of fifty—a new junior partner with the firm of Davis, Dash & Youngblood. Ian Renfrow. Tall, dark, relatively handsome. She'd met him at the firm's Christmas party, a social duty she'd been unable to decline. As the sole beneficiary of the vast Colfax conglomerate, she was DDY's top client.

So-o-o, she brooded. *Ian Renfrow*. He'd spoken with her for some time at the party and even escorted her through the buffet line, but she hadn't heard from him since. Would a professional man who'd expressed no particular personal interest send his firm's most important client such an extremely unprofessional valentine? It didn't seem likely.

Unfortunately, there was no one else. The only other men she came into regular contact with were the doormen downstairs, a suspiciously flamboyant florist, a museum director and, lately, the two carpenters who were building her new greenhouse on the roof. One of the carpenters was very large and very male in a bristly, burly, blue-collar sort of way. They'd exchanged greetings in the kitchen once when he was on his coffee break and she'd wandered in for a snack. Her hello had been bashful, his greeting gruff, practically a growl—and that was the extent of it. Not in any way memorable.

Charlotte touched one of the delicate pastel petals of the *Phalaenopsis* orchid set to the side of the desk. If the brush with the carpenter wasn't memorable, why had she recalled it so clearly?

With an effort she focused on Ian Renfrow. Even though his chin was a bit weak and his conversation rather dry, he still might have the élan to be her secret admirer. But was it even remotely possible that he had been charmed by quiet, plain, sedate Charlotte Colfax?

She couldn't imagine that it was.

Finally there came the sound of the mail sliding through the brass slot on the front door. It hit the Persian carpet with a soft thud. Charlotte had to restrain herself from running out to the foyer like a child on Christmas morning. Hattie Connor, the housekeeper, would notice her eagerness. And rousing Hattie's curiosity was best avoided.

All is normal, Charlotte said silently. Anticipation flickered inside her. *Outwardly*, she amended, *all is normal.*

2

A LONG TEN MINUTES LATER, Hattie made a token knock on the half-opened pocket doors and entered the library. With her rosy cheeks, deeply creased laugh lines and figure like a feather pillow, Hattie could have been a gentle, motherly type of housekeeper if someone had rememered to tell her to conform to the role. Instead, when her short curls had begun to gray, she'd dyed them an improbable copper color with faint undertones of green and orange. Beneath her standard-issue apron, she wore neon-colored sweatsuits or loud floral polyester combinations. She was nosy, hard working, sympathetic and opinionated. In other words, a substitute mother. Charlotte loved her.

The anonymous valentine would be just to Hattie's taste, a rare savory tidbit in the sameness of her charge's unexciting, not-so-private life. Which was why Charlotte didn't intend to share it. In this case, she would relish her privacy.

"Good morning, Hattie," she said, striving to keep her eyes away from the stack of mail in the other woman's hand.

"Mmm." Hattie stopped, the mail still held out of Charlotte's reach. "Not working today?"

Charlotte ignored the dark computer screen and unopened research tomes. "I'm taking a break."

"You must be sick." Hattie dropped the mail on the desk and pressed her plump hand to Charlotte's forehead. "I've never known you to miss a morning's work unless you're sick. Like your father, you are."

Charlotte pried the older woman's hand away. "I'm not ill. Truly." Nonchalantly she reached for the mail.

The housekeeper's eyes narrowed. "You're flushed."

Charlotte waved airily. "It's nothing."

"Um-hmm." Hattie edged around the large cherrywood desk, her interest sharpening as she scanned Charlotte, the room, then Charlotte again. She scratched her elbow contemplatively.

Even though Charlotte had instantly spied the corner of a mottled vellum envelope, she made herself select one bearing the Colfax College logo, and wave it in the air. "Another letter from Dr. Alcorn. Shall I read it to you?"

Hattie wrinkled her nose. "I'd rather eat my dust mop."

Charlotte laughed lightly as she unfolded the pages.

"The man's a buffoon." Hattie snorted, tossing her curls so their green tinge caught the light. After Dr. Alcorn's first visit, she had made it clear that she considered the English Lit expert an insufferable prig, wasted on Jane Austen, the household's good china and especially Hattie's world-famous lamb stew. Aside from which, she was indelicate enough to point out, he was old enough to be Charlotte's father. "Soup's on at 12:30—don't be late," she said, and made a hasty escape.

At the moment Dr. Alcorn's advanced age was the furthest thing from Charlotte's mind. As soon as Hattie left the library, she ripped open the foil-lined vellum envelope and pulled out the card, a duplicate of yesterday's, decorated with intricate lace-patterned velvet hearts. The message inside picked up where the last one had left off.

See it draped golden over your bare breasts

Charlotte gasped. *Bare breasts?* she thought in alarm. *Bare breasts?!*

Why, as far as the outside world went, Charlotte Colfax—reclusive, refined, restrained Charlotte Colfax—did not even possess bare breasts!

Trembling, she closed the offending card, then two seconds later opened it again. From memory, she mentally grafted the first anonymous message onto the second:

I want to feel your hair sliding through my fingers like silk
See it draped golden over your bare breasts

Charlotte's hands continued to shake even when she folded them together tightly in her lap. She could not seem to comprehend that someone she knew—or someone who knew her by sight, at the very least—had dared to send such an audacious valentine. The presumption of it was astonishing. And the suggestion, the blatantly erotic suggestion—!

She was…overcome.

But also intrigued, she realized. Gradually she began to wonder, and imagine, and picture…picture, well, certain *things*. Sexy things. Things she hadn't considered in so long that her body was awakening in a tingling rush that was quite thrilling. The warmth in her cheeks spread through her veins like a potent aphrodisiac. Amorous possibilities suggested by the black velvet valentines worked their way into her consciousness, almost as if they belonged there.

Her hair.

His hands.

Her *breasts?*

Oh, yes, she was intrigued. Helplessly, hopelessly intrigued. Tomorrow's mail couldn't come soon enough.

CHARLOTTE RECEIVED TWO telephone calls late that afternoon. The first was from Ian Renfrow's secretary, who wanted to make an appointment concerning a legal problem that had cropped up with one of the Colfax subsidiaries. To Charlotte, it sounded like the sort of detail she paid her lawyers not to bother her with. She was about to put off the appointment until she realized that it might be Ian's first overture to furthering their acquaintance. *Not counting the valentines,* she thought pleasurably, and said an almost enthusiastic yes to a Friday lunch date in DDY's corporate dining room.

She was noting the appointment on her calendar when the telephone shrilled again. Dr. Hadley Alcorn was calling from Colfax College with the news that he would be in the city for a three-day weekend conference. He was free on Friday afternoon and would be most pleased to grace Charlotte with his presence. She plotted swiftly and invited the professor to her apartment for tea, although without the enthusiasm with which she'd welcomed the upcoming meeting with Ian Renfrow.

It was not until she'd hung up and returned to her calendar that she realized Friday was Valentine's Day. *Valentine's Day,* and she'd just made plans with two eligible single men—either of whom could be her anonymous correspondent!

Charlotte rose from the leather chair and began to pace the silent library, toying with her pearls as she weighed the likelihood that one of the invitations was no coincidence. After going so long without considering the opposite sex as such, she was suddenly besieged with possible suitors. And what's more, she was actually enjoying it.

Absorbing as the subject was, eventually Charlotte stopped and looked around her as if seeing the room for the first time. She shivered. The fire had nearly gone out; the coffered ceiling, dark cherry paneling and shelves of books seemed to press in on her, inducing claustrophobia. She thought of the kitchen. It was always the warmest, homiest room in the cold, stone-walled apartment.

The housekeeper was carrying on a jovial conversation with the carpenters, who sat at the marble-topped island in the center of the room. The bigger guy's manly rumble of a chuckle ceased abruptly at Charlotte's sudden appearance. She hovered in the doorway. "Excuse me."

Hattie was something of a flirt; entertaining two men at once had her round face flushed with pleasure. "Oh, dear, oh, dear me," she said, her giggles overriding Charlotte's soft-spoken arrival. She flapped her apron. "You're a rascal, you are. A regular charmer." With a wiggle of her cabbage-rose-clad rump, she turned to take a pan of cornbread out of the oven.

Charlotte wasn't sure which of the carpenters was supposed to be the charmer. They'd both gone silent as they rose to greet her, the younger, bearded one swiping off his fur-lined cap with a hand the size of a bear paw.

He was massive, a Paul Bunyan in the flesh. Well over six feet. A very large six-and-a-half, Charlotte estimated, with a muscular breadth to match his height and a chest that in its heather gray flannel shirt looked as wide as the East River. Her gaze lingered for a moment, then dropped to his hands. The knuckles stood out like small rocks embedded under weathered skin, but at the same time his fingers were surprisingly gentle and deft as they folded the bill of the cap. This gave her pause until she remembered that he did, after all, work with his hands....

She studied his downcast face. While he could not be called handsome, he was utterly masculine. A strong nose, a broad forehead, the rampant, untamed hair that seemed to grow in all directions. But she was surprised to see that a faint ruddiness stained his cheeks above the scruffy brown beard. Was *he* shy, too? Not a characteristic she'd normally associate with a man so large and powerful.

Perhaps it was her presence that was the inhibiting factor. Charlotte hesitated, aware that her position as "princess of the castle" had dampened the trio's casual camaraderie. There had been a time when Esme would have admonished Charlotte for getting familiar with the hired help. But that time was past, Charlotte remembered gratefully. Even if she was awkward about it.

She attempted a smile, trying to put everyone—including herself—at ease. "So," she said. "How—how is work progressing on the greenhouse?"

The older, grizzled carpenter nodded soberly. "Just fine, Miz Colfax. We'll be setting the rest of the glass on Monday."

They'd been in and out of the apartment for three weeks now, and suddenly Charlotte had forgotten their names. *Stupid girl. Don't you ever pay attention?* "That's good," she said, straining to remember. "Gil?"

The older man nodded again.

Charlotte's glance flickered toward the younger carpenter and caught him watching her from beneath his thick eyebrows. Something about the rich, velvety brown of his eyes—and the intensity of his regard before he looked away again—knocked her off-kilter. Her heart gave a hard thump in her chest, and suddenly her brain was spinning like a gyroscope falling off its axis, the words inscribed in the black velvet valentines whizzing around and around her head.

He couldn't be...no, no, the very notion is absurd. He couldn't. He's much too shy. Charlotte stepped back, found the edge of the marble countertop and clutched it.

Then again, the valentines *were* anonymous.

"Quinn," she blurted, suddenly thinking of his name. She didn't know if it was his first or last; he'd been introduced simply as Quinn.

Slowly his eyes lifted to meet hers, and she felt the question in them. It was not a cool, professionally detached sort of look, but one that was personal and gently probing. Gently probing...

Charlotte wasn't sure how to explain herself, so she resorted to the first excuse that came to mind. "I wondered if you could work tomorrow. Either of you. I know it's Sunday. I'll pay overtime. I'm..." She swallowed, feeling flustered, overheated. All because of two valentines that were probably only a bad joke. "I'm just so eager to get my orchids into the new greenhouse," she finished, her voice flagging.

The carpenters glanced at each other. "Well..." Gil said, hesitating.

"I can do it," Quinn volunteered. His voice was deep and resonant, like playing the left-hand keys on a piano with the pedals pressed to the floor. Charlotte's scalp tingled. "I'll be glad to."

"Why, that's..." Charlotte stopped to inhale; she'd sounded all breathy, which was inappropriate whether or not her stepmother was there to scold. "I'd appreciate it," she said more smoothly. But now it was she who couldn't meet Quinn's eyes. *What if—?*

Hattie wiped her hands on her apron, her gaze switching back and forth between them like a horse's tail. "Hmm," she murmured. There were no flies on Hattie Connor.

Gil said, "I can come for a few hours, Miz Colfax. Quinn'll need a hand with the glass."

Charlotte found herself beaming, even though she wasn't sure what she'd done, or why she'd done it. "All right. Thanks." Irresistibly drawn, her eyes coasted up Quinn's impressive length one more time and came to a screeching halt when they met his curious stare.

Out of reflex, she checked her hairpins. Crow's-feet crinkling, his eyes deepened with a silent amusement that gave her a jolt of recognition.

She colored. Maybe Quinn wasn't so shy, after all.

3

LATE THE NEXT AFTERNOON, Charlotte sat on her queen-size bed and lined up three identical black velvet valentines before her on the Italian tapestry coverlet. This being Sunday, the third card had not come in the mail but had been hand-delivered by the doorman, catching Charlotte by surprise. Luckily, Hattie, who lived in, had gone off with a friend to a matinee movie, and so missed the reaction Charlotte hadn't been able to disguise and the agitated questions she'd thrown at the dumbfounded doorman.

Many minutes later she was still pink in the face and twittery with nervous excitement. Unable to resist the cards' allure, she wiped moist palms on her thighs and opened them one by one.

I want to feel your hair sliding through my fingers like silk
See it draped golden over your bare breasts
Twine your pearls around my hands and roll them over your naked, twisting body

Hugging herself for comfort—and a degree of control—Charlotte read the cards again. And again. She gnawed at her lip, disturbed by the unseemly warmth growing inside her. How could she welcome such presumption?

Well, obviously she *could.* Judging by her swelling eagerness, she *did.* The better question was if she should.

She shouldn't. But she closed her eyes anyway and let the vividly disturbing images sweep through her like a fever. She began to hum under her breath. And to sway.

Mmm, yes, she could see them—a man's hands, large hands, so large...looped with the ropes of her pearls, making a slow, erotic journey over her wanton body. And, oh, my, how she would moan, aching with desire, needing to move as his hands pressed against her, the pearls smooth and round and cool, but growing warmer as they rolled over her flesh, Quinn's callused fingertips grazing her tender nipples so gently, so roughly, so sweetly—

Charlotte's eyes popped open. *Quinn!*

Had she abandoned hopes of Ian Renfrow for Quinn, the carpenter, a man even less likely than Hadley Alcorn? Was she losing all reason? All her inhibition?

Actually, Quinn wasn't as far-fetched a candidate as Dr. Alcorn, or even Terrence, for that matter. But he was certainly less...appropriate.

A short, shocked laugh flew from Charlotte's mouth. How completely ridiculous. *None* of this was likely— much less appropriate. Especially not for an uptight princess who'd been closeted in her castle for nearly two years.

Still, there were the black velvet valentines. Three of them now. Three times someone had sat down and thought of her as he wrote out his most intimate thoughts....

Charlotte's heart contracted. If only there actually was a man out there who'd play prince to her princess. He didn't have to be a storybook hero on a white charger. He didn't have to be handsome or rich. She wanted a real man with a princely soul, someone strong and daring and courageous and true, someone who would love her. The sort of man she could love in return, unconditionally.

Before the black velvet valentines had arrived, Charlotte had thought her life was set. She was doing okay— not necessarily fulfilled, but content. Even though she continued to miss her father, she kept herself busy with her scholarly work, the three afternoons a week she volunteered at the museum, and the greenhouse full of delicate orchids and other exotic flora that took such painstaking care. Hers was a quiet life, very quiet, and she liked it that way. She *was* content.

Or at least she had been until the black velvet valentines had arrived and turned her perceptions inside out.

That was it. She felt turned inside out, as though all the emotions and physical yearnings that she'd kept contained were suddenly exposed to the world, let loose to run amok. It was unsettling...and at the same time strangely freeing. The echoes of her stepmother's constant admonitions—*Sit still! Be quiet! Don't touch!*—were lost on the new, excitable Charlotte Colfax. Which was quite wonderful in an unfamiliar, thrilling way.

The questions remained, though. Who was her black velvet prince? Was he a prince at all?

Charlotte scooped up the valentines and hid them in a locked drawer of the special lapis lazuli treasure box she'd had since childhood, the repository of everything from charm bracelet trinkets to several mediocre love poems by Terrence White, written before he'd left Colfax College to travel cross-country as an itinerant poet, as he'd put it. Or a penniless bum, as Esme had put it when she was urging Charlotte's father to forbid the relationship.

What Charlotte needed was advice. Hattie was at hand, of course, and obviously willing to speak her mind, but she was too close, practically a mother. That wouldn't do. Charlotte needed the kind of advice only a girlfriend could give.

She reached for the telephone on the bedside table. It might take some wangling to squeeze time from her friends' schedules, but a judicious hint of her black velvet surprise would do wonders. And a reservation at a favor-

ite Columbus Avenue bistro for an early dinner. Valerie
loved to dish gossip and Lynne loved to eat.

THE THREE WOMEN hadn't seen each other in many weeks,
so their first twenty minutes together were taken up with
settling at a table beneath a vintage tin ceiling, exchang-
ing compliments over how great they all looked, exclaim-
ing over pictures of Lynne's babies and ordering from a
snooty waiter who seemed put out by Valerie's asking
how the coq au vin was prepared and Lynne's instructing
him on how it *should* be prepared.

Charlotte sat back and smiled at the goings-on. She'd
met Lynne when they were students at Colfax College in
Massachusetts, three years apart, the ex-and future girlfriends of the same romantic, long-haired, ill-fated under-
graduate, Terrence White. Lynne's tastes had evolved
since then; she was now a do-it-all superwoman with a
psychiatrist husband, two adorable children and a highly
successful career in banking.

Valerie, on the other hand, was a pampered socialite
with a highly successful bank balance, a standing appointment with a psychiatrist, and two adorable Lhasa
apso dogs she called Gucci and Pucci. "And there's also a
husband," she sometimes said with droll sarcasm, "in
that order."

As different as the women were from each other, and as
much as they'd been drifting apart, Valerie and Lynne
were still Charlotte's closest friends, her unofficial big sisters. They'd been a vital support system during the worst
days of her father's fatal accident and funeral and her
subsequent move back to the city.

Once they'd been served their appetizers, Charlotte
tentatively elaborated on her news about the black velvet
valentines. Valerie and Lynne were so flabbergasted they
couldn't speak—a rarity. To fill the silence, Charlotte revealed her thoughts on the identity of her secret admirer.

Lynne was the first to recover her aplomb. She picked up a small wedge of smoked duck and goat cheese pizza and eyed it suspiciously before popping the whole thing into her mouth. She chewed carefully, then with more enthusiasm as a nod of approval became an expression of bliss. "I'll tell you one thing, Charlotte," she said thickly, reaching for more of the appetizer, "it's definitely not Ian Renfrow. Not a chance in a zillion." Seeing that her friend was taken aback at the blunt assessment, she swallowed and offered Charlotte an encouraging smile. "Not because of you. Because of your money. No attorney is going to risk losing the Colfax retainer over a few funny valentines."

Valerie nodded. "I'm afraid Lynne's right. And I should know." Her marriage to a high-profile, big-ego defense attorney had soured not long after the splashy society wedding.

Charlotte frowned. "How can you be so sure? The valentines were anonymous. Maybe he doesn't intend to reveal himself—ever."

Lynne flipped her napkin. "Then what's the point?"

Thoughtfully Valerie nibbled off the point of a triangle of grilled eggplant pizza. Her almond-shaped eyes were cunning when she turned them on Charlotte. "What exactly did these valentines say?"

Charlotte, predictably, blushed. "They were, um, rather, umm, *suggestive.*"

"Definitely not Renfrow, then," Lynne said, with the air of a woman who'd learned to thrive in a man's world where the dollar was king. As always, she looked sleek and professional in one of her classic business suits accented by a no-nonsense wristwatch and plain gold wedding band.

"Can you be more precise?" Valerie tilted up her chin and let out a throaty chuckle. The fine gold threads in her of-the-minute designer sheath glistened when she shimmied her shoulders. "Or more explicit…if that applies?"

Embarrassed, Charlotte buried her face in her hands.

"You're such an innocent," Valerie scolded. "Locked away in that Upper East Side castle with the family retainer and a hothouse full of orchids."

Lynne's eyes rolled. "Those turrets! Ye gods!"

"The torches and tapestries in the lobby. The fireplace big enough to roast a fatted calf. The portraits of dear, departed Gottfried, and all the other dead Colfaxes." Valerie shook her lush auburn curls, maintained by a team of hairstylists. "It's all so dreadfully Gothic. Not to mention symbolic."

"I know, I know." Charlotte was remembering why she'd stopped asking her friends to the apartment. Although they thought The Castle was a hoot, by visit's end Charlotte invariably wound up feeling hopelessly outdated. "Still, I grew up there," she said. "It's where I feel closest to my father…my parents. I can't just move—"

"Your father wouldn't want you to grow mold, either."

"Put Hattie out to pasture." Valerie pulled no punches. "Get on with your life. Let down your hair. Find a man— one who's not afraid to show himself. Have a fling, or at least one good f—"

"Let's not be hasty," interrupted Lynne. "Charlotte's not you, Val. She has standards."

Although Valerie drew herself up haughtily, the banter was too familiar for any of them to take offense. In the triangle of their friendship, Lynne was always the practical, efficient one, Valerie the sophisticate with an earthy badgirl streak, and Charlotte was the sweet innocent whom Lynne defended from Valerie's attempts at corruption.

Glumly Charlotte took a bite of the pizza. She, for one, was tired of her role. Chewing, she told herself that the black velvet valentines were her best chance to break out of character. All she had to do was let herself be seduced.

That was *all?* Just thinking of the huge risk it would entail made her throat close so tightly she almost choked.

"Look at that expression," crowed Valerie. She clapped her hands in delight. "Finally! The princess wants to climb down from her tower and do the nasty."

Charlotte sputtered.

Smiling kindly, Lynne pressed a glass of wine into her friend's hand. "No, I don't think so. Charlotte's just ready to be someone's valentine."

"Someone's *wicked* valentine," Valerie insisted.

Charlotte looked at them over the rim of the glass. She drank deeply and set the wine down, unable to hold back her sheepish grin. Lynne was right, but so was Valerie.

"We've got to figure out the identity of the secret admirer before you commit to anything," Lynne said as she reached for the remaining slice of pizza.

"It can't be that dorky professor." Valerie shuddered. "Perish the thought."

"Dr. Hadley Alcorn," Lynne said. "He was old even when I was a freshman."

Charlotte cleared her throat. "He's probably in his late fifties," she calculated. "Which I'd wager is not too old from the male point of view."

Valerie, older than Charlotte by nine years, sniffed petulantly; she'd begun collecting plastic surgeons' business cards when she hit thirty-four and found her first tiny wrinkle. "Being surrounded by nubile young coeds tends to give a man grandiose ideas."

"God, Charlotte, Alcorn's practically bald." Lynne winced in disgust, even though her husband's forehead was advancing at a rapid pace. "He wears rumpled shirts and suspenders and hunches over his desk like—ugh— Larry King. And have you forgotten how he used to blow his nose and swig cough medicine behind the podium during lectures?"

"He has allergies," Charlotte said, to be fair. "He can't

help it. He's a nice enough man, otherwise. Quite sincere. Very polite and earnest."

"Don't tell me—"

"You can't possibly—"

"No." Charlotte was firm. "I am not interested in Hadley Alcorn. Not that way." She thought uncomfortably of their Valentine's Day tea. Dr. Alcorn could take the invitation as…an *invitation.* "But what if he's interested in me?" she asked, her voice gone thready.

"There's got to be someone else," Valerie said.

"Anyone else," Lynne pleaded.

"Well…" Charlotte thought fleetingly of Quinn. "What about Terrence?"

"Good old Terrence." Lynne shrugged. "I suppose it's possible, but isn't he still hitchhiking in Sweden or Lapland or someplace like that? I heard that he's writing an epic ode to the midnight sun."

"Maybe he's back," Charlotte said, without much hope. She was grasping at any explanation but the one that was beginning to seem the most attractive.

"This is your mutual college boyfriend, the rambling poet?" Valerie asked. "The one who took bribe money from Charlotte's stepmother and absconded to Europe in style? Sounds like a loser to me."

"That's right." Lynne nodded cheerfully. "The man who was my college fling with bohemia was also Charlotte's first love. Terrence might have been a loser, but he was a charming loser. And very good-looking, too. A real heartbreaker, but in the end still a toad."

Charlotte cringed at her friends' pithy summations. Even though she wasn't carrying a torch for Terrence, the memory of how she'd been burned by him and Esme was still sore.

Belatedly realizing this, Lynne patted Charlotte's hand.

"I certainly hope you're not wishing that Terrence has come back. Especially after what he did to you last time."

Charlotte squared her shoulders. "Not at all. I just can't think of anyone else who..." Again, Quinn passed through her mind.

4

CHARLOTTE'S INSTINCT had been to keep him private, but now she wondered if she was also keeping his secret. With his callused hands, dirty overalls and caveman hair, he wasn't the type about whom her sophisticated friends would have an open mind. An inappropriate college fling was one thing; developing actual *feelings* for a tradesman was another.

Valerie took one look at Charlotte's expressive face and pounced. "Okay, princess, give it up. Who is he?"

Charlotte remembered that she had come to them for advice. "The carpenter," she mumbled reluctantly.

Simultaneously, Lynne said, "Pardon?" and Valerie said, "What!"

"The carpenter."

"What carpenter?" they squealed.

"His name is Quinn and he's been building my new greenhouse. I don't really know him, but he's..." Charlotte drew in a breath, trying to find the right words to explain her curious attraction to Quinn. "Well, he's a big man. Muscular. Kind of unpolished. I—I've talked to him once or twice and I...sort of like him." She bobbed her head. "Yes. I do like him."

"A carpenter?" Lynne said doubtfully. "Not your type."

"A carpenter," Valerie mused. She licked her lips. "If he's a strapping fellow, as you say, better built than your brick outhouse, then there's no reason he couldn't be at least your *temporary* type, hmm?"

Wordlessly Charlotte shook her head. She didn't care to dissect her fledgling feelings for Quinn. Nor did she want to subject him to Valerie's analysis of his physical attributes. Which were plenty, she thought with private satisfaction. Her friends didn't have to know the details.

"I don't see it," Lynne said. "A guy like that..." She shook her head. "Not for Charlotte. She's too fragile."

Consternated, Charlotte insisted, "No, I'm not."

"It would be an experience," Valerie said slyly. "Which she's sorely lacking."

"Carousing with the carpenter is not the way to go about gaining experience." Lynne was starting to sound like a stern older sister, a role she played well. "If you really think he might be sending the valentines, Charlotte, I'd advise you to nip him in the bud—"

Valerie chuckled. "Sounds kinky."

Lynne scowled. "Cut him off at the pass, then. You don't want to encourage this sort of thing. It's just not like you."

Though Charlotte nodded, inside she was wondering how Lynne could know such a thing when she herself didn't. For nearly two years she'd been cocooned inside The Castle, healing herself, yes, but maybe growing, too. Evolving.

There was no telling who she'd be when she emerged.

THE SUN HAD SLIPPED low in the sky by the time Charlotte returned from the restaurant. Quietly she let herself into the apartment and climbed the stairway to the roof. It was her habit to watch the sunset from the western tower. The carpenters would have gone home by now. Having been too embarrassed by her provocative assumptions about Quinn to face him earlier that day, she'd kept to the library instead, where she was safe. Always safe. Habits were hard to break, particularly when it hadn't yet occurred to her that she no longer wanted to be safe.

The February wind whipped across the turrets, throwing back the hood of Charlotte's green cashmere cape, catching at loosened strands of her hair. She pulled the cape tighter and picked a path among the leftover bricks and stones and the litter of the new construction.

Quinn and Gil had done a good day's work at her whim. The hexagonal greenhouse was fully enclosed, faceted like a diamond, although the glass panels were still opaque with condensation. Charlotte had splurged on a glorious Victorian leaded-glass dome to crown the structure, and inside would be teak tables and shelves for the plants, a herringbone brick floor and an old, mossy fountain that had been shipped overseas from her father's ancestral home in Germany.

Charlotte had every reason to be pleased. Just the same, she paused doubtfully, her thoughts taking an unexpected turn. Yes, the greenhouse was almost finished, but when it was, Quinn would leave. A frown marred her smooth brow. She might never know if he'd been the one to send her the valentine cards. He wasn't; she was sure he wasn't. In fact, she shouldn't even be entertaining the possibility, but still...

Charlotte shook her head vigorously, as if the motion could dislodge her wayward wishes instead of only loosening her French twist. She put her hands to her hair. Ah, well. There was no one around to care if her hair became tangled and messy. Certainly not Esme.

Walking toward her usual place in the wide curve of the turret, Charlotte plucked out a few of her hairpins. The twist collapsed against her neck in a heavy coil. An ominous wind whistled through the openings of the crenellated stone wall, rising as she threaded her fingers through the twisted skein, freeing the long strands—

"Your hair is beautiful."

Charlotte jumped. The hairpins flew from her fingers,

several falling with metallic *pings* against the stones, the rest flung over the parapet by the wind.

"Oh!" she said haltingly. "Oh—my. I didn't see you." Although she'd recognized Quinn's voice instantly, she was overwhelmed by the strangeness of his large, foreign, *male* presence. Pleasantly overwhelmed, it seemed.

He bent to pick up the pins, avoiding eye contact. "I was inside the greenhouse, just finishing up." He wore a sheepskin coat that hung open over his dirty denims and low-slung tool belt.

The wind tore at Charlotte's hair; she pulled up her hood to contain it. "When I asked you to work today, I didn't mean for you to stay so long...."

"I wasn't planning to charge you by the minute, ma'am."

"It's not that. I just don't want to impose."

"No problem." He held out the hairpins.

She looked, wide-eyed, but didn't take them because she didn't quite dare to touch his hand. It was so large, twice the size of hers. Capable of...who knew what?

"I think..." Quinn said cautiously, finally bringing his gaze around to meet hers, "I think I stayed so late because I was waiting for you."

Her throat closed. "For me?"

"I knew you'd be up here at sunset."

Frozen, stunned, she squeezed the words out. "How did you know?"

"I've seen you, several times." He gestured toward the street. "Usually from down below, as I was leaving. But once I was here. You didn't notice me—I was off to the side carving out a tricky spliced joint. So I kept quiet. I didn't want to disturb you. I..."

Charlotte had closed her eyes as Quinn's deep voice washed through her, but when it trailed off she opened them again. He'd slid his hands into his jacket pockets and hunched his mountainous shoulders. His head was bowed, the tips of his ears flaring as pink as the underside of the clouds that streaked the sky behind him.

He *was* shy. Which meant that even though he'd seen her with her hair down, he'd never have written, much less mailed, such provocative valentines. Particularly not to someone like her. Charlotte blinked several times, her eyes tearing in the wind. Was she disappointed?

Yes.

"I thought you probably wanted your privacy," Quinn concluded.

He might look like a burly, rough-and-tumble lumberjack, but there was more to him than that. Facets unexpected, unexplored. She was drawn to him, wanting to discover all the small details about him, the sort that were fascinating only to...lovers.

"Oh, well," she said at last, when their silence had stretched out too long. "I suppose you're right. It's my habit to take a few minutes to—" *dream* "—to myself—" *as if she hadn't already spent the day alone!* "—at the—the end of the day."

He nodded, seeming to understand more than she'd said.

Charlotte turned away, narrowing her eyes against the gray winter light so that Central Park's bare, frost-whitened trees and the flat silver coin of Turtle Pond became a Currier and Ives print. The familiar view brought her back to herself.

With a shrug she purposely relaxed her hold on the collar of the cashmere cape. Quinn was just a nice, normal guy; this was just a nice, normal conversation. Nothing intimate about it. "I come up to the roof all the time. I used to play here when I was a little girl." She indicated the curve of the tower wall. "You can see why."

"Castles and kings," he said, a faraway look in his eye. Then he glanced at Charlotte, at the spill of her hair. "And princesses, too."

She whispered, "Oh, yes," and flushed, wondering if he had also read her mind those times he'd caught her daydreaming in the sunset.

The wind gusted, flapping her cape, whipping her hair across her face. She started to claw at it, but suddenly Quinn was there, his big hands smoothing back the fly-away tresses.

Charlotte went very still. His roughened fingertips brushed her cheeks. So gently. Her face lifted to meet his touch. She swayed toward him, her lips parting....

His voice was rich with wonder as he rubbed a strand of her hair between his fingers. "It's like spun gold."

Her eyes flickered with alarm. *Gold? Did he say gold?*

Quinn backed off. "Sorry."

Charlotte bit her lip, unable to think of a response. Not when the renewed possibility of his being her mystery correspondent was pounding through her like the beat of a jungle drum. With fumbling fingers she gathered up her waist-length hair, tucked it down the back of the cape and drew on the hood. She was flush with what could only be called anticipation: her skin was suffused, her lips moist and full, the peaks of her breasts drawn painfully tight beneath layers of bothersome clothing. An overreaction, she avowed, but still one she couldn't prevent. The black velvet valentines had brought her to a fever pitch of need, with the prospect of the days to come only heightening the torture.

Four days to go till Valentine's Day and already she wanted to pounce on the carpenter simply because he'd brushed her hair out of her face.

Unaware of Charlotte's quandary, Quinn had shoved his hands back into his pockets and returned to a safer topic. "As a kid I played in the alleyway behind my mom's fourth-floor walk-up. The only castle I had was a dumpster. But it wasn't so bad," he hastened to add when

Charlotte's brows knit with concern. "There was also a tree. An imaginative kid can do a lot with a tree."

She made a brave face. "Then I'm glad you had a tree."

"Eventually my friends and I foraged enough wood to build a tree house." His face was turned toward the park, but he seemed to be watching her from the corners of his eyes. He smiled, his beard ruffled by the wind. "It was almost as good as your castle."

"I'm certain it was." She'd played often in her rooftop castle, until Esme had arrived with her rules about proper behavior, and her punishments if they should be disobeyed. Charlotte sighed. Since few children were "lucky" enough to inhabit The Castle, playmates had been scarce, particularly those who could meet Esme's strict requirements. The complaint seemed trivial compared to Quinn's story.

"Didn't have much of a view," he murmured. "Not like this."

The building's view was worth a million dollars, literally, but Charlotte preferred its intrinsic value. Even when she felt most confined, there was always the majestic view from the rooftop to expand her outlook. She relied on it.

But was that also why she'd allowed her life to narrow so drastically since her father's death? Had she forgotten that a view was in the end only a view—not a substitute for living?

And a wistful wish for fulfillment would forever remain elusive. Unless she actively sought to make it come true.

"Charlotte?" Quinn said, his low voice a pleasurable counterpoint to the keening wind. "I mean, uh, Ms. Colfax?"

She glanced shyly at him. "Charlotte, please. Call me Charlotte."

"Would you like a tour of the greenhouse? It'll get you out of this wind."

Beyond the Manhattan skyline, the sky was darkening its reds to purple, its rosy pinks to gray. Lights were blinking on up and down the Upper East Side, festive as Christmas, gaudy as the Fourth of July. Charlotte's spirits rose like a flag flying from the ramparts. *I can do this*, she thought. *I can be friends with this nice, normal, thoughtful man.* It didn't matter whether or not he'd sent the black velvet valentines.

"Yes, please," she said to Quinn. Oh, yes, *please.*

5

Quinn had remained a perfect gentleman throughout their brief tour of the greenhouse. The only moment that seemed at all inordinate was when she pointed up at the Victorian glass dome and her cape swung open, revealing the length of her hair and the double string of pearls that had looped itself around her right breast. For one fleeting moment Charlotte thought she saw the kindling of desire in the carpenter's expression. The breath went out of her like a burst balloon. But then she pulled the cape closed and he blinked and looked away. An instant later she convinced herself that she'd imagined his reaction because she'd *wanted* to. In actuality, Quinn appeared to be unaffected by her out-of-use charms. He showed her the teak benches that were soon to be installed and the fountain still in its packing crate, and that was it. They'd said a decorous good-night and gone their separate ways.

A connection, Charlotte decided as she entered the stone foyer the next morning, her footsteps echoing up to the vaulted Gothic ceiling. A small, human connection. The kind of contact she'd been sorely lacking since her self-imposed exile from the world.

But it wasn't anything else. It wasn't *more*, regardless of how many times she recalled the touch of Quinn's hands on her cheeks. Or fantasized about the heat and hardness of his big, furry body as it enveloped hers—

She made herself stop. Even though the black velvet valentines had done quite a number on her libido, she didn't have to succumb to every preposterous soap bubble fantasy that floated down the pipe. Her suddenly overactive imagination had latched on to Quinn because he was at hand. Period.

Wheeling an upright vacuum, Hattie crossed the far side of the foyer. Quickly Charlotte opened one of the drawers of a heavy, carved-wood console, trying to look as though she had a reason to. With only a cursory glance, the housekeeper slid open the pocket doors and entered the rarely used but immaculately kept living room. Charlotte exhaled in relief.

She replaced the fountain pen she'd blindly withdrawn and shut the drawer. Her reflection in the large Venetian rococo mirror over the console caught her eye: the upswept hair, pale skin and cautious blue eyes, the nose that was as straight as a ruler and a fraction too long, her unpainted lips and long neck twined with pearls, the expensive but understated lamb's-wool sweater and skirt, served well by the perfect posture that had been drilled into her by dance teachers. Outwardly, she looked the same.

Inwardly, she was a stranger to herself, fizzing with emotions she scarcely recognized.

At last she saw the mail slide through the slot in the door and fan across the carpet. She scooped it up. Hattie charged into the foyer a beat too late. She followed Charlotte into the library, anyway, bouncing on the balls of her feet as she tried to see past Charlotte's shoulder. Obviously, Hattie sensed there was something terribly interesting about the mail.

Nonchalantly Charlotte tossed the envelopes on the desk where her computer sat cold and silent, which in itself was enough to raise the housekeeper's curiosity. She met Hattie's sharp look with a bland smile and sauntered out of the room.

Locked in her bathroom suite, Charlotte sat on the padded stool by the vanity and withdrew the envelope she'd slid under the waistband of her skirt, away from prying eyes. For a moment she held it flat between her palms, letting anticipation do its shivery thing to her insides.

Mmm...

She slit the flap with her thumbnail. It was the same style of envelope, the same card. Black velveteen, lace-patterned hearts on a dusky pink background. Inside was another of the handwritten notes:

Watch your eyes get bright
Your lips go soft
Your skin glow pink in the candlelight

"Candlelight," Charlotte whispered in awe, slowly raising her eyes—gone bright as jewels—to the vanity mirror. *What was he planning?*

For that matter, what was *she* planning?

As always, Charlotte was drawn to the rooftop at sunset. For once, however, the appeal was not the view, or even her inner dream scape. She wanted to see Quinn.

"Hi," she said, finding him inside the greenhouse, polishing the glass. She held up a thermos of hot chocolate. Hattie's sly offer of hand-painted mugs, cloth napkins and cookies on a tole tray had seemed too fussy for a supposedly impromptu visit. "Do you like hot chocolate?"

He plucked off his hat. "I like it when Hattie makes it. Her recipe puts those packets of chocolate-flavored powder to shame."

"Instant hot chocolate?" Trying to appear unaffected by his deep, rough voice, Charlotte matter-of-factly unscrewed the cap and poured. "I've never had it."

"Lucky you."

"Hattie and her home cooking have been with us since my...since I was six." Charlotte swallowed past the lump in her throat. "Since my mother died."

"I'm sorry. That must have been rough."

"Oh, well..." She studied the interior of the greenhouse. "It was so long ago, I've almost forgotten what it was like to have a mother. I do have vague memories of tea parties, bath time, bedtime stories. Hugging her good-bye..." Charlotte blinked.

Quinn was watching with concerned, melting eyes. "Do you mind if I ask how...?"

When Charlotte compressed her lips and shook her head, he understood that she meant she didn't want to talk about it. Instead he turned away to point out the stonework along the northern walls of the greenhouse, new since her last tour. "The stonemason will finish to-morrow, then we'll have the plumber in to complete the hookup. You'll be operational by this weekend."

"I've been keeping most of my orchids in one of the guest rooms with the heat turned up. Sometimes I run the shower to raise the humidity...." Needing the distraction, Charlotte prattled on without caring what she said. More than almost anything, she wanted to feel Quinn's strong arms around her as his gravelly whisper reverberated in her ear. She wanted heat and comfort and partnership—a need that, for a change, was not prompted by the erotic valentines.

Quinn sipped the hot chocolate, his Adam's apple bob-bing like a cork in the sturdy column of his throat. A thatch of brown chest hair curled from the open collar of his chambray shirt. There was something primitive about his furriness, something that revealed in Charlotte ele-mental urges heretofore unknown. Which was still shock-ing to her, but not as much as it had been.

"Tell me about yourself, Quinn," she said, trying to stanch her rising hunger, the kind that *was* prompted by the valentines. "You don't seem like a New Yorker. I keep picturing you living in, oh, a cabin in the woods, some-thing like that."

He fingered his beard. "Because I look like a lumber-jack?"

Her composure cracked with a giggle. "You do! Like Paul Bunyan."

"It's my winter disguise," he said. "Come spring, the beard'll start to itch and I'll shave it all off."

Without concealing her interest, she studied what she could see of his face, trying to decide how he'd look clean shaven. In the thicket of his overgrown beard, the corners of his lips—they were firm, shapely lips—tucked up into a self-conscious grin.

Charlotte made herself look away, first at the antique fountain, partially uncrated and spewing excelsior, then up at the overhead watering system suspended from the ceiling. A kind of cozy warmth was seeping through her—the coals beneath the hot blaze of her attraction to Quinn. They were a pair, she thought with a silent laugh—two unassuming people hiding beneath scads of hair.

Except that, insofar as the valentines went, she was beginning to assume a whole lot....

"There's not much to tell about myself," Quinn said. "I'm a pretty simple guy. What you see is what you get."

"Everyone has a story."

"I suspect yours is more interesting."

Her hand waved. "Poor little rich girl? You've heard it all before." She sat on one of his handmade teak benches and trailed her fingertips across the satiny wood. "Tell me how you became a carpenter."

He leaned against the brick wall that enclosed the staircase, one knee drawn up so his jeans tightened around his muscular thigh, which was the size of a tree trunk. Charlotte doubted she could span it with both hands, but, oh, she did want to try. An odd little feeling bubbled inside her at the image that made in her mind. How lascivious!

"You're right, Charlotte," he said, and she yanked herself back into the conversation. "I was born in Minnesota. To an unmarried eighteen-year-old with dreams of dancing on Broadway. We moved back and forth between New York and a small town in the Minnesota Iron Range—the city when my mom had a job or a boyfriend, the country when she was flat broke and desperate enough to move back in with her folks." He stopped, looking surprised at himself for having said so much.

Charlotte put her elbows on her knees and prompted him with a nod.

"So…" He scratched his beard. "As a kid, I started to pick up spending money by scavenging discarded furniture, fixing it and selling it to secondhand shops. Then when I was old enough, I worked construction, where I met Gil. He's a master carpenter—took me on as an apprentice. Eventually we became partners, and—" Quinn gave a self-effacing shrug "—here we are. I told you it wasn't much of a story."

"It's a pretty impressive story." Charlotte nipped at her lower lip. "In fact, you're a pretty impressive guy," she said all in a breath-held rush, just to get it out. "And I have to go," she added, just as quickly. She stood, picked up the thermos, dropped the plastic cap, let out a groan and got down on her knees to search for it where it had rolled under the bench.

So did Quinn. Charlotte pulled back an instant before their hands touched, then regretted her timidity.

"Here you go," he said hoarsely, and fitted the cap to the thermos and gave it a twist as Charlotte slid her index finger up the handle to brush the side of his hand. The overture was not very significant, but she felt almost daring for attempting it.

Quinn's thick lashes lowered. "Charlotte?"

"I've never—never…" She shook her head, amazed at herself, yet determined to go on. "I've never kissed a man with a beard before. And soon it'll be spring and you'll shave and then…"

He leaned back on his heels and said quietly, "Go ahead."

She hesitated, wishing that he had taken the lead. How could she—?

Like this. With a shaking hand she reached out to touch the wide expanse of his chest. On contact, fascination began to overtake bashfulness; she pressed her fingertips into him. He felt so hard, like the stone walls of her castle. But warm, too, in a way that made a similar warmth pool thickly in her, down low, where she ached to have him filling her. His hardness, huge and hot inside her…

Charlotte inhaled sharply. Her nostrils flared, filling with his scent. Resin and wood shavings and leather, and beneath that, a warm male musk that sent her senses spinning. She had to close her eyes to regain her balance. Maybe this was all a dream.

When she opened them again, Quinn still hadn't moved. He knelt there on the bricks, huge and solid and hirsute as a grizzly bear. But still. Patient. Waiting for her touch. Her kiss.

Almost disbelieving what she was doing, Charlotte leaned forward and lightly touched her lips to his. It was a brief kiss, only long enough for her to register the fleeting sensation of his breath fanning hers, the pleasant shock of his warm lips and the tickle of his curly beard grazing her face.

No tongue or aggression. No pressure. No doubt.

Only an overwhelming sense of wonder and grace.

"JUST A MOMENT, young lady," Hattie called across the dim foyer. By her tone, she meant business.

Charlotte halted beneath the portrait of Gottfried Colfax, the Goth descendant who had founded the family dynasty. Every time she looked at him—stern, glowering, aggressively ugly—she felt that she was letting down her ancestors. Even a round Irish housekeeper in fuchsia velour sweatpants and orthopedic shoes could intimidate Charlotte Colfax.

Hattie waved something in her hand. "What's this, then, Charlotte, me darlin'?" The high, skeptical arch of her brows matched her voice, not her words.

Charlotte saw with a sinking dread that the housekeeper held the fifth black velvet valentine. In her rush to get to the museum on time, Charlotte had left it on the desk. Right out in the open.

Worriedly she wound her pearls around one finger. "Why, that's a valentine, Hattie." She would try and brazen it out.

The housekeeper flipped the card open and purposely popped her eyes. "'Delectable'? I can't imagine what *that's* supposed to mean!"

Funny. I can. Very easily. But now was not the time. Charlotte suppressed her wilder imaginings and tried to remember if she'd left the envelope on the desk, too, or in the wastebasket. And even if she'd thrown it away, would Hattie still find it?

Charlotte decided to take the chance. "I was going to write a Valentine's Day verse. For Lynne's kids." On a black velvet valentine? Better not give Hattie a chance to think about that one. "But I didn't have time to finish, so—" Charlotte snatched the card "—thanks. I think I'll take this with me and mail it from the museum. See you."

Hattie scowled as the door slammed. *"Delectable?"* Charlotte heard her say, even through the thickness of a heavy wooden door banded in steel.

Charlotte answered in a whisper: "Yes."

Yes, yes, yes! The answer escalated inside her as the elevator descended toward what would be a lobby in any other building, but in The Castle was a grand entrance hall with a massive fireplace, faded tapestries and a platoon of round-the-clock doormen to play palace guard.

It was all very oppressive, but Charlotte didn't care; she was on the verge of escape. She smoothed her hands over her suede slacks, almost preening.

Someone, somewhere, thought she was *delectable*.

6

BEFORE CHARLOTTE LEFT the museum for the day, she often stopped in one of the galleries to have a look at her favorite painting. Consumed by her own thoughts, she was almost upon the man standing in her way before she looked up. "Quinn!"

He turned away from "her" painting and said, "Charlotte," with such obvious pleasure that she rocked back on her heels, warmed to the core by the candor of his welcome, but suddenly also wondering if this meeting was a bit *too* coincidental.

"I'm surprised to see you here," she said.

"Oh? Yeah." He buttoned his sheepskin coat as if he meant to leave. "Gil and I finished early at the greenhouse, so I stopped here on my way home to look at a few paintings. I wasn't—"

"I wasn't—" Charlotte said at the same time.

They laughed self-consciously. "I wasn't implying that you were slacking off on the job," she explained. His surprise at bumping into her seemed genuine; she must have leapt to another mistaken conclusion. Seeking distraction, she glanced at the painting. Even though it was small and murky with age, not even a wide, carved, gold-leafed frame could overshadow its quality. "This is my favorite painting."

"It's very peaceful."

"Serene," she said.

"But..." Quinn hesitated, his eyes deepening as he

studied the painting. "Mysterious, too. Portentous. So rich it's...sensual."

"Yes, exactly!" Charlotte blurted excitedly, surprised once again by Quinn. A strolling security guard frowned, but her lowered voice retained its marvel. "I always feel that there's so much going on in this painting that we can only guess at. All the underlying emotions and hidden meanings." The painting was a simple enough scene: a blond woman in black with a white collar, seated at a desk, reading a letter in the buttery sunlight flooding a small, square window. "What's beyond that doorway?" Charlotte mused. "See how she's torn the envelope, as if in a rush to open it? It makes me wonder about who has sent the letter. What has he written?"

When she realized the implication of what she'd said—particularly if Quinn was sending the valentines—she took a step back, suddenly nervous about seeing him again. The last time they were together she'd kissed him. And he had held himself in check beneath the featherlight stroke of her touch.

"Look at the way the light pools on the wood of the desk," Quinn said, still absorbed by the painting. "And there's a glint in the woman's eye, even though she looks so demure. I always imagine that the letter is from her—"

He cast a quick look at Charlotte and altered his expression. "From her beau," he said mildly, thrusting his hands deep into his pockets. The air was thick between them; they both knew he'd intended to say *lover*.

"Well, I'm finished for the day." Charlotte managed to make a flurry out of arranging her cape and checking her purse for gloves. "It's time to head home."

"You work here?"

"I'm a volunteer. Several afternoons a week I sit in a little cubbyhole upstairs and coordinate the volunteer fundraisers." She glanced again at the Vermeer painting. It was not considered to be the most outstanding piece in the Dutch artist's oeuvre; how interesting that both she and Quinn had picked it out—and were affected the same way. Particularly in light of the black velvet valentines. "Do you…come here often?"

"Not often. Occasionally." He smiled fleetingly. "I suppose I don't seem like your usual sort of patron of the arts."

"Not at all." But she was prevaricating, backpedaling. It was too easy to see only Quinn's outward appearance and overlook other qualities—such as his gentleness, chivalry and artisan's skill—that were less obvious. "We get all kinds."

He shrugged and extended his hand. "May I walk you out?"

Charlotte knew her mismatch with Quinn would cause a minor sensation and rampant speculation among the museum staff. So she gave him a demure smile and said, "Yes, thank you."

"I WANT THE TASTE of you in my mouth," Charlotte said experimentally. Her mouth filled with lukewarm water. She swallowed and ducked beneath the showerhead, letting the hard spray cascade over her until her hair was soaked through to the scalp. She swiped the dripping strands out of her face.

I want the taste of you in my mouth, she repeated silently. Her stomach clenched.

When the sixth black velvet valentine had come that morning, she'd thought she was ready for anything. Apparently not. The question of exactly what part of her the secret admirer wanted to taste was thought provoking, to say the least. And fantasy invoking—to say the most.

Charlotte turned her face up to the spray. Water droplets pelted her eyelids, her lips; she parted them, thirsting for the kiss of a man who could be literally anyone, except that he was always someone very like Quinn in her imagination. The meek little peck she'd given him the other night was beginning to seem inconsequential. What she was feeling now could be satisfied only by a long, hot, driving kiss. A rapacious kiss, a knock-me-flat-and-make-love-to-me kiss.

No, she decided. Not *a* kiss. Kisses, many of them. A thousand kisses, all over her body, and when she returned the favor she'd taste herself on his lips. But she'd taste him, too. *She'd have his taste in her own mouth.*

Charlotte ran her hands across her wet belly, down her slick flanks. Even bathed by the warm, soothing water, her skin still blazed with desires, cravings...for Quinn's stare, his touch, his potent kiss. Tentatively she touched herself, wishing it was him. Unsatisfied, she slipped her hands through her hair, lifting it off her neck, arching her back so the water sprayed her breasts. His hands on her breasts, she thought, slowly sliding her palms over them in languid circles. Her nipples tingled, tightened. *His mouth. Everywhere.*

So much pleasure. If only...

Throbbing, hollow, needy, she touched herself again, still wishing it was him. *Quinn.* The name had become a vital part of her vocabulary.

But when she opened her mouth to say it out loud there was only water, drumming against her face, pounding at her naked body. Warm, wet, pulsing...but not nearly enough.

She wanted more.

"WATCH OUT, CHARLOTTE," Lynne said over the telephone. "I don't mean to insult you, but this Mr. Valentine could have more on his mind than romance and seduction. You're wealthy, single, with no close relatives. Ripe picking for a sly opportunist."

Charlotte gaped at the receiver.

"It's something to consider," Valerie agreed. Charlotte

had called Valerie first, needing to talk, hoping for sympathy and maybe encouragement. Valerie had suggested they make a conference call to Lynne. A power chat, she'd called it.

Hah. Apparently her friends thought Charlotte was not only powerless, but naive and gullible, to boot. Even as Charlotte made a face at the phone in her hand, she had to admit she understood why Valerie and Lynne might have reason to feel protective. They didn't know how different she was inside. How *empowered*, she felt.

By lust, she added with a silent yearning. Why weren't her friends cooperating?

"Not that you shouldn't carry on," Valerie continued. "Use 'em and lose 'em, that's my motto. Don't get emotionally involved and *never* open the checkbook."

"Really," Lynne said. "May I remind you this is Charlotte we're talking about? Charlotte and some fly-by-night carpenter who may or may not be a gigolo—"

"He is not!" Charlotte interjected.

"Whatever," Lynne said. "Just drop him, Charlotte. And do it fast."

"*After* you've gotten your kicks," Valerie added.

"You don't know Quinn," Charlotte said, seething at the various insinuations. She sat on her bed, wrapped in a terry-cloth robe, her wet hair making a damp swath down her back.

"I knew *Terrence*," Lynne countered.

"They're not the same," Charlotte said. "Quinn isn't—he absolutely isn't like Terrence! He's honest and kind and really rather shy. I doubt that he sent the valentines...." The heat in Quinn's expression when he'd seen her pearls looped around her breast rose from Charlotte's subconscious, but she pushed the image back down so she could continue. "I wish he had, though! I truly do. He might not be sophisticated or moneyed or socially acceptable, but he's a good man. I think that counts for a lot."

She was winding down. "In fact, I would be darn *lucky* if he wanted me...."

Lynne cleared her throat. "Then that settles that."

"I had no idea," Valerie murmured. Her tone seemed to suggest that Charlotte's vehemence was less palatable than her own jaded outlook.

Somewhat shocked herself, Charlotte tugged her robe a little tighter and tucked her damp hair behind her ears. *Well.* She'd called her friends with questions of what she should do and whom she should do it with, but clearly she'd already known the answer.

TOMORROW WAS Valentine's Day. Charlotte put her elbows on the desk and shifted in the leather chair, wondering if "Mr. Valentine" would finally reveal his name. It would be a bad joke on her if he turned out to be a man she scarcely knew, or even a stranger off the street. A stalker, a Peeping Tom, a pervert.

Goodness, no, she thought with some alarm. If the mystery man was anyone but Quinn, the black velvet valentines would suddenly seem distasteful. Even Ian Renfrow or Hadley Alcorn, the only other viable candidates, had become unsuitable to her. Perhaps she should cancel their appointments....

And then what? Charlotte stopped herself from reaching for the phone. She could see herself sitting alone on Valentine's Day as usual, only this time it would be worse because she would know and care about what she was missing. Then again, what could she do to prevent such a dissatisfying outcome? It wasn't like Quinn—or whoever—had made a tangible romantic overture. At this point the valentine messages were still as ephemeral as her daydreams.

It was possible, even likely, that the erotic journey of the black velvet valentines would lead nowhere except to her own big, cold, empty apartment and her own big, cold, empty bed.

"Knock, knock," Hattie said, and shoved open the heavy pocket door with a special verve. "We have mail."

Charlotte's stomach dropped. Hattie was beaming, presenting the morning mail on a silver platter so pretentious it was ridiculous, the likes of which had not been utilized since Esme's day. The seventh valentine was placed prominently on top of the small stack of mail as if there could be any mistaking it.

"I believe it's a valentine," Hattie said, sotto voce. Her eyes sparkled.

Charlotte tried to smile. Dear Hattie. She meant well, and she was obviously thrilled that Charlotte had a suitor, but she had no idea of the valentine's contents. And it was going to drive her up the wall when Charlotte declined to share.

There was no avoiding the situation. Carefully Charlotte picked the vellum envelope off the platter as though she wasn't dying to rip it open. "Thank you, Hattie. Why don't you, oh, take the rest of the day off? In fact, why don't you take a long weekend? Go and have an extended visit with your sister in Boston. I can manage till Monday."

"Heavens, no! There's the tea to get for Dr. Alcorn, and I have plans myself for Friday evening."

"You do?"

"With me darlin' sweetie pie, Everett, of course. Just the usual turn around the neighborhood, probably stopping for a bite." Everett was Hattie's gentleman friend of long standing. He was a widowed dry cleaner, as short and stout and good hearted as Hattie. On occasion Charlotte wondered if the pair would ever marry, but, unlike Hattie, she wasn't one to pry.

Funny thing, though. At least for the moment, *Hattie* was being unlike Hattie. Normally she'd have been crowding closer, practically climbing into Charlotte's lap to read the valentine. Instead she was behaving almost discreetly.

Charlotte turned the envelope over in her hand, thinking of Hattie and her cozy coffee klatches with Gil and Quinn. Could the housekeeper be privy to more information than Charlotte herself?

But Hattie could hold back no longer. "Jumpin' jelly beans, Charlotte! Aren't you going to open the darn thing?"

Charlotte glanced up sharply. That was more along the lines of what she'd expected. But now what? She shifted again in her father's chair, trying to come up with an excuse to get rid of the other woman.

Hattie heaved a dramatic sigh. "I suppose you want your *privacy.*"

Charlotte blinked in surprise. "If you wouldn't mind…?"

Hattie turned on her heel and left the library, muttering something about there being limits on how much privacy was good for a person. But she'd gone so easily that Charlotte's suspicion remained piqued. She tried to take it as a good sign—the valentines were from Quinn, and Hattie, in on the secret to some extent, approved.

Charlotte looked at the envelope with blossoming anticipation. She decided to take it to her bedroom, where she was less likely to be disturbed. Let Hattie draw her own conclusions.

Charlotte's bedroom suite wasn't as dark and heavily furnished as the rest of the apartment. Only the outer wall was made of the blocks of granite she found so oppressive. When she'd moved back in almost two years ago, she'd stripped the draperies with their swags and fussy passementerie off the tall, narrow windows and replaced them with diaphanous, royal blue silk panels that floated in the breeze. Workmen had torn away the patterned wallpaper and painted the walls a shade of blue that was as soft and pale as a daydream. They'd rolled up the old rug, polished the harlequin black-granite-and-white-marble floor, carted off the dark wood furnishings and moved in the dainty cream-and-gilt French pieces Charlotte had chosen for herself. The bedroom had become a space where she could really breathe. And let down her hair, so to speak.

Ignoring the sitting area, Charlotte got the valentines from the lapis box and crawled onto the high bed she'd had since her childhood. The blue toile de Jouy fabric that was draped from a gilded "crown" near the ceiling gave the bed a grand scale. It was the centerpiece of the room, a bed fit for a princess.

A girl could dream, couldn't she?

Not when she's twenty-five, Charlotte told herself. Twenty-five was well past the age of consent—time to grow up and be a woman. Dreams were nice, but dreams were no longer enough.

It was time. She shuffled through the black velvet valentines. There were seven of them now, a week's worth of sweet, tantalizing torture. She didn't have to open the cards to read the contents; she'd memorized them without trying, repeating the words to herself at night. Every night.

I want to feel your hair sliding through my fingers like silk
See it draped golden over your bare breasts
Twine your pearls around my hands and roll them over your naked, twisting body
Watch your eyes get bright
Your lips go soft
Your skin glow pink in the candlelight
Delectable
I want the taste of you in my mouth

Charlotte opened the seventh valentine.

Your velvet warmth wrapped around me like a glove as you take me deep inside

"Oh, Quinn," she breathed, praying that he was her suitor. He had to be. She wanted no other.

She repeated the seventh message to herself, imagining the press of Quinn's large body on hers, the exquisite invasion as he entered her. His size was frightening, and exciting. He had such a controlled strength, like a wild animal on a leash. Beneath his outwardly gentle manner she sensed a strain of hot-blooded carnality. That made her smile. Considering the valentines, there'd pretty much have to be.

Because Charlotte trusted that she'd ultimately be safe with Quinn, she wanted to release the beast in him. On her. She wanted to experience hot, wild, rapacious sex and have it still be making love. She might not know Quinn well, but she knew enough to believe that he was a man who could deliver both.

Oh, yes. Brushing her fingertips over the valentine's velveteen flocking, she whispered his erotic words to herself one more time.

A sound she'd never heard before, a deep, humming note of pleasure, rose from her lips. She sank into the pillows, her body gone into a languorous, liquid recline. Heat and pleasure and desire rolled through her like the tide: relentless, pulling, inexorable…a force of nature. Having no choice, she went with it, twisting against the pillows, running her hands up her body until they were pressed to her cheeks, where she could feel the blushing warmth that swelled her veins. Her skin, her heart, her soul were suffused with longing, the sweet, aching longing of her dreams.

But the hot charge of electricity that made her hips squirm deeper into the mattress was lust. Pure animal lust.

Charlotte tunneled her fingers through her hair, wrenching it loose from its restraints. She was free. She was on fire.

She was ready for her black velvet prince.

_____ **7** _____

THERE WAS NO BLACK VELVET valentine in Friday morning's mail. Charlotte couldn't quite believe it. She flipped through everything, even the catalogs, carelessly allowing other letters and assorted junk mail to drop to the Persian rug.

Nothing! Charlotte slammed the remainder of the mail onto the console. How could he quit today, of all days? She glanced up and away, then returned to stare, astonished at what she saw in the mirror. Her eyes were glowing, wide as a madwoman's. Her lips were soft and darker than normal, like ripe plums. Her hair remained unbound, hanging in disarray to the small of her back. When she'd heard the mail arrive, she'd run barefoot out to the foyer in only a gray silk slip. The straps had fallen off her shoulders; her breasts were nearly bursting from the lacy bodice.

Charlotte almost laughed. She looked every bit the strumpet who'd just wakened from a night of bawdy entertainment. It would have been funny if she hadn't actually spent the night alone.

Hattie appeared and knelt to pick up the pieces of mail that had been tossed aside. She made a _tsk_ing sound at Charlotte's appearance, but declined comment.

Charlotte had her own built-in system of recrimination; it was starting up again inside her head. _Look at you, running after the man like a common tramp. Have you no pride?_

"The card will come," Charlotte said, blocking out the voice. "It's not meant to end this way."

"Ahem."

Charlotte started. Now she'd gone and done it. "Y-yes, Hattie?"

After a long, measuring silence, in which Hattie surely must have battled her tart tongue, she settled on a mild question. "Shall I help you dress?"

Like a princess with a handmaiden? Grudgingly Charlotte smiled at the picture. Hattie wasn't the type. As for herself...who knew? "No, thank you," she said. "But you may call for a cab."

"A woman telephoned this morning from DDY. They're sending a chauffeured car at eleven-thirty."

So she was getting the top-drawer treatment. "Fine," Charlotte said, but she couldn't help wondering if Ian Renfrow would pop out of the back of the car with a bottle of champagne and a dozen red roses. She certainly hoped not. "Well, then, maybe I should get dressed."

Hattie's head bobbed. "That might be a good idea." There was only the slightest tinge of curiosity in her voice. She didn't even seem to think it odd that her modest employer was running around in a flimsy silk slip.

Charlotte peered at the housekeeper. "Are you feeling all right, Hattie?"

"Never better."

"Glad to hear it. Tell me, are Gil and..." Charlotte's eyes went to the mirror. "Are Gil and Quinn at work on the roof?" She'd managed to say Quinn's name without changing expression. The wilder impulses of her animal attraction to him were suitably contained, but wreaking havoc on her nervous system.

Although it might have been Charlotte's imagination, it seemed that the curve of Hattie's scarlet lips was knowingly smug. "Prompt and diligent, the pair of them," the housekeeper said. "That fellow Quinn's a man to depend on."

Charlotte managed a nod before she flew toward her

bedroom like a bird from a cage. She didn't want to know what Hattie had meant by such a statement. She only hoped the woman was right.

"HAVE THERE BEEN ANY deliveries?" Charlotte asked the instant she walked in the door after her dull luncheon meeting with Renfrow. She stamped her boots on the stone floor. "Faxes? Phone calls? Singing telegrams?"

Hattie chuckled as she helped Charlotte off with her long coat. "What in the world has gotten into you, Charlotte Colfax? It's not like you to be so jumpy."

Charlotte was roiling with pent-up frustration. "It's Valentine's Day, Hattie. Have you forgotten?"

"Seems to me *one* of us has forgotten more Valentine's Days than I can count on my thumbs." Hattie brushed a few flakes of snow off the champagne-colored fake fur. "Why should this year be any different?"

Charlotte had no acceptable answer. "It just is, Hattie." Her shoulders slumped as she unwound a fringed blue scarf from around her head. High on the wall, Gottfried Colfax scowled down at her. "It just…is."

Clucking like a mother hen, Hattie took the scarf and gave Charlotte a little shove. "Go and get yourself warm by the fire. Running around to lawyers' offices is no way for a lady to spend her Valentine's Day."

Charlotte went into the library. "You can say that again," she muttered, holding her hands out to the flames crackling in the arched opening of the granite fireplace. Her lunch with Ian Renfrow had been a bust, even though, technically, that was what she'd wanted. There had not been a hint of romance in the air, just boring business talk, salmon with snow peas and reams of paperwork for dessert. Ian—he'd unbent enough to ask her to call him Ian—had been courtly, it was true, but also dry as toast. The only sign that anyone at the law firm knew this was Valentine's Day had been the red roses in the bud vases on each table in the corporate dining room. Hardly enough to make a woman's heart leap with joy.

Scratch Ian Renfrow off the candidate list.

WHATEVER HER FEELINGS about the professor, Hattie put on an impressive tea. They had finger sandwiches and an assortment of petit fours and iced cookies, as well as two fragrant blends of hot tea. Dr. Hadley Alcorn was clearly flattered by the spread, and by the show Hattie made, bobbing in and out of the library with another plate of sweets and many small attentions to the professor that were so saccharine Charlotte's teeth ached. Alcorn mistook this for solicitude; Charlotte knew it was merely interference. Hattie didn't want to leave Charlotte at the professor's mercy should the rash romanticism of St. Valentine make him lose his head.

Not that Alcorn's intentions were anything less than noble. Charlotte had understood that fact as soon as the professor came through the door in a starched shirt—barely wrinkled—and his finest tweeds—only slightly frayed—bowing and scraping in honor of Charlotte's surname even though she had no actual power or influence over the college that employed him. It was the portrait, she decided. The redoubtable Gottfried Colfax inspired much tugging of the forelock in men like Hadley Alcorn.

"Charlotte." Dr. Alcorn snuffled into his linen napkin, adjusted his glasses and sent a doe-eyed look across the tea table. "You may have deduced that this visit is not without purpose."

Abruptly Charlotte lowered her cup of mint tea, missing the porcelain saucer entirely. Tea spattered the tablecloth. "I hadn't—I didn't—" She sat up straight, shot through with alarm. The torpor produced by the warmth of the fire and too much rich food and placid conversation had vanished. "Dr. Alcorn...?"

"Please, allow me a word." The professor held up his

hand, revealing a cuff edged with cream cheese. "I imagine a young lady of your station must deal with this sort of thing quite often. I shan't be tedious about it."

The black velvet valentines had been anything but tedious. And Charlotte refused to link them with the small, bald, untidy man sitting across from her. Absolutely!

"Dr. Alcorn, I really must say I'm surprised that *you*—"

He honked into the napkin.

Charlotte winced. Searching for words, impossible words, she nervously ran her fingers up and down the length of her pearls. "For you to come here and—and…" She stopped, stricken to the quick; the situation was hopeless.

Alcorn reached past the teapot and captured Charlotte's hand between his. "My gross assumption is unpardonable, I know," he crooned, petting her knuckles. "Charlotte, sweet. Lovely, lovely Charlotte. If only you knew how I've wrestled with this decision. I didn't want to sully your innocence with my—"

"Dr. Alcorn!"

"With my, er, *needs*," he finished. He made a puppy-dog face at her as though expecting her to console him for his struggle.

Charlotte's mind was spinning. She thought she might faint out of sheer horror. "Please don't," she whispered, wrenching her hand free.

Alcorn shook his head. "I must. The times we live in have forced even I, a scholar and man of integrity, to stoop so low. My proposal to you is one of…"

Proposal! Charlotte's dreams shattered under the blow. If only she could tune out the professor entirely in order to preserve some shred of her dignity. Where was Hattie when she needed her?

"…Valuable research that must continue, whatever the cost.…"

Charlotte blinked.

The professor droned on. "...The necessity of mercenary concerns, so at odds with high-minded scholarship...."

Relief hit Charlotte like a bucket of ice water. "You're asking me for money?" she said. "Good lord, you're asking me for money!"

Shamefaced, Alcorn ducked his head. "My approach has been unforgivably crass, I know."

"And your proposal?"

He brightened. "To continue my studies. An extended sabbatical in the British Isles will be necessary. Your patronage would guarantee a certain degree of...comfort."

Charlotte was so astonished by her deliverance from the brink of disaster that she rashly promised him full funding. She could think of only one thing.

Scratching Dr. Hadley Alcorn off the candidate list left just one man. And he was up on the roof, exactly where she had always dreamed of finding her prince.

CHARLOTTE WAS AGHAST. "Let me get this straight," she said to Hattie. "Quinn left early?"

"And Gil, too," the housekeeper said, calmly nodding her brassy curls as she packed tiny cakes into a plastic container.

"They both went home?"

"Yes." Hattie stacked several boxes of leftovers and put them in the refrigerator.

"Why?" Charlotte cried plaintively. If she hadn't been so accustomed to restraint, she'd have raised her hands to the ceiling and howled.

Hattie was being stubbornly phlegmatic. "Because the greenhouse is finished, of course."

"That's just great." Charlotte was sure that she'd never be able to take any pleasure in using it. Not now. Thunderstruck by Quinn's abandonment, she walked out of the kitchen without noticing Hattie's secretive little smile.

Later, in her dressing room, Charlotte stripped away the charcoal gray business suit and then the lacy underthings she'd thought would be a sexy surprise to her seducer. Hah!

She'd been drifting aimlessly around the house, unable to settle in one spot. Even after going over and over the situation, thinking about the black velvet valentines, she honestly couldn't come up with any other candidates. Well, except for laconic Gil and the doormen downstairs, she supposed, though that was sheer desperation.

How could Quinn have gone home without—without...

Without *her*. Didn't he know she was his for the taking? Didn't he want her?

If not for the proof of the valentines, she might have believed the whole affair was a product of her overwrought imagination.

Perhaps because even now she still had some faint hope of salvaging her Valentine's Day, she chose a pair of luxurious black satin hostess pajamas from the closet and slipped into them. The wide bands of black velvet trim on the sleeves and pants and cowl collar made the ensemble an especially ironic choice. Charlotte summoned up a hollow laugh. If her mystery man should decide to deliver the final black velvet valentine in person, she would be ready.

Her heart leaped to her throat when a knock sounded on her bedroom door. She raced to answer it. Before she could, Hattie poked her head inside. Charlotte skidded to a stop, swallowing her last, desperate hope. Of course Quinn wouldn't come to her bedroom.

Hattie stared at the glamorous hostess pajamas. "I'm off to meet Everett, Charlotte. Is there anything you need before I go?"

Charlotte smoothed one hand over her hair until it met the resistance of the large, tight knot of her bun. Suddenly she wanted to rip out the combs and pins that held it in place and toss them *all* off the roof. "I'm fine, thanks," she told Hattie. A fine liar.

"Nice outfit." Hattie clucked. "But it's cold out there. Remember to put on a coat when you go up to the roof."

In the pit of Charlotte's stomach there was a stirring of something that felt a lot like hope. "The roof?" she whispered.

The housekeeper's smile quickened Charlotte's reaction. "Don't you always go up to the roof around this time?" Hattie asked with a shrug. "Why should today be any different?" She gave the black satin-and-velvet pajamas another long, approving look and then waved goodbye.

Dazedly Charlotte lifted a hand to return the wave. Maybe Esme had been right; she *was* a stupid girl. Of course Quinn wouldn't come to her room.

He would meet her on the roof.

THE MAN IN THE GREENHOUSE was a stranger to her.

Charlotte stopped in her tracks and released the breath she'd held climbing up the stairs to the roof.

The stranger turned, elegantly dressed in black, as tall and large as Quinn, with the same chestnut shade of hair, but not—

"*Quinn?*"

She recognized his smile. "Gave you a shock, didn't I?" he said, self-consciously rubbing a hand over his clean-shaven jaw. His hair was tamed and trimmed as well.

"It must be spring," she said.

He gestured at the greenhouse. "Looks like it to me."

It was a relief to let the transformation of the greenhouse occupy her attention for a minute. Before she could look at Quinn again, she needed to adjust to his shocking metamorphosis from caveman carpenter to black velvet prince.

All her orchids, camellias and other flowers, along with the trees and plants, had been moved from the spare bedroom. They filled the greenhouse with their lush colors and scents and greenery. Just as dazzling was the soft glow of candlelight illuminating the glass hexagon. White candles were everywhere—lining the benches and tables, scattered randomly on the brick floor, even hung from the ceiling in sparkling glass globes. Tiny votives followed the curved stone enclosure of the pond, whose surface rippled under the gentle stream of water burbling from the mossy lion's-head fountain. A small patio table and chairs had been set up nearby. Wide-eyed, Charlotte took in the bottle of champagne and crystal flutes, the extravagant box of chocolates, the bouquet of perfect pastel roses with a creamy-gold vellum envelope propped against the vase.

The black velvet valentine.

Charlotte's emotions billowed. Without thought, she floated toward the table, moving so lightly she may have transcended gravity. Her open coat dropped from her elbows and slid off her forearms, making a puddled rug on the brick floor.

"So it was you," she whispered, tracing the envelope with one fingertip.

Quinn didn't speak until she looked up at him. "Yes, it was me," he said, and she felt his voice reach deep inside her, the promise of it filling her heart, the timbre of it sending shivers over her skin.

Even though his face was unfamiliar, in her heart she'd known him all along. He was...princely. Her eyes welled.

"Forgive me if I was being pushy."

Charlotte dashed a hand at her tears. "Certainly!" she declared with a shaky laugh. "I—I've never...well, I mean, nothing like this has ever happened to me, and I..." Her cheeks grew warm, but she held her gaze steady on his face. "I loved it."

He stepped closer. "It started as an impulse, out of the times I saw you standing in the turret, looking like a beautiful, sad princess. Your hair…" Tentatively he reached out to touch it. "Like I said," he murmured. "Spun gold."

"I didn't know what to think when I got the first card." Charlotte was rattled, but she closed her eyes and started to quote the familiar, almost comforting words. "'I want…'" Her throat clenched; she couldn't go on.

Quinn picked up the line. "I want to feel your hair sliding through my fingers like silk."

Hearing the words she knew so well spoken in his alluringly roughened voice could have been an out-of-body experience, but it wasn't. It seemed perfect, exactly right. Desire was in her like the warm glow of a fire in a potbellied stove.

She gazed at Quinn's face, too fascinated to let her shyness prevent an intense examination. Without the scruffy beard, mustache and long hair, he was better looking than she'd expected. But all that was irrelevant. In her eyes, Quinn would forever be magnificent because he had opened up her world. He had reached past her defenses and touched her heart.

She stroked his cheek. It was smooth, soft, new. A muscle ticked beneath her fingers as his jaw tightened. His eyes were hot and fierce on hers. Still a leashed beast, she thought, even with his slick new veneer. She took her hand away, catching her breath as the familiar animal attraction flickered inside her, licking her erogenous zones with flame.

"I wasn't going to reveal myself, ever," he confessed. "But then, well, I started to get to know you. And I thought…" He stopped, conflicted. "I don't know. Maybe it was foolish, but I thought there might be a chance you could care for me."

"More than a chance," she said, but still he seemed unsure. Charlotte knew the feeling, the self-doubt. "Tell you what," she ventured. "Let's make this night special. Just let go and give in to the magic without question or recrimination. Believe in our instincts, not our doubts."

Boldly Quinn met her searching gaze. "Do you know what you're saying?"

She did, but the thought of it made her mouth go dry and her voice freeze up in her throat. She managed a nod. It was enough.

For all his size, Quinn could move like a cobra when he wanted to. In a split second Charlotte was caught up by him. His large hands were in her hair, cupping her head as his mouth covered hers. Willingly she surrendered to the deep, sucking pull of his open mouth and invading tongue. Heat rose inside her until she was dizzy with it. She leaned toward him and his tongue plunged deeper and her need grew so immense she succumbed to it without struggle—a glorious, sinking, swooning sensation that brought her snugly into Quinn's strong arms, pressed to his wide chest. His rough tongue made a broad, licking stroke along the arch of her throat, over her chin, and stopped to lap at her open mouth. Deliberately, he tasted her, like a big cat with its paws wrapped around a bowl of cream. And when he pulled back to regard her broodingly—perhaps covetously—she knew that he wouldn't stop with only one taste.

Prickling with anticipation, she continued to study his unfamiliar face—up close this time. It wasn't finely chiseled or pretty-boy handsome; it was hard and rugged and blunt, as if cut from rough stone, seasoned to a harsh masculine beauty by work and struggle and integrity. The beard had been only a distraction, not a disguise. Without it, he was less obviously a tradesman—especially in his black woolen turtleneck and tailored trousers—but still essentially the same.

A working man, built like a fortress, stalwart and true. A man to count on.

A man to love.

8

MATTHIAS QUINN WAS NOT the kind of man who expected rewards to come his way without cost. He'd always scrambled and fought and worked hard and long for everything he'd achieved, from turning his first job as a gopher into a master carpentership, to the painstaking renovation of his Brooklyn town house, to the college degree he'd recently earned at age thirty-three after eight years of night school. To have a woman like Charlotte Colfax in his arms because of a few daring words and fancy phrases was a minor miracle.

She seemed to have no understanding of why she'd inspired his worship. That in itself was one of the reasons he found her so engaging. She was natural, unaffected, good-hearted—completely unlike what he would have expected from an Upper East Side heiress.

"Quinn?" she said, her smoky blue eyes grown so solemn he cursed himself for hesitating. The housekeeper, Hattie, had revealed some of the details of Charlotte's situation. Her air of loneliness and silence tugged at Quinn's heart. He'd always been a soft touch for street beggars, runaways and mangy alley cats. Strange to think that Charlotte Colfax had needs, too, needs that Matthias Quinn, out of a city of millions, might be able to meet.

He wanted to. Very much.

It was truly a miracle that he'd have the chance to try.

"Charlotte," he said, almost reverently speaking her name. He stroked her shoulders.

Her eyes flashed, surprising him. She was not as docile

as her manner suggested. "Don't start treating me like a princess *now*," she said. "Not after…everything. I don't want to stay locked in my castle tower!"

"No," he said, an agreement.

"Then…would you kiss me again?"

She pressed herself softly against him so that he felt the subtle sway of her breasts and, under his palms, the impatient shift of her shoulder blades. He traced a fingertip over the delicate line of her collarbone and she lifted her face, her lips asking for his as she went up on her toes. She wanted to be seduced. Who was he to refuse?

His hands slid up to her magnificent hair, its color too rich to have come from a bottle. Charlotte's long gold hair had been a beacon the first time he'd spotted her atop the castle tower at sunset. She had been such a sight he'd wondered that the entire city hadn't come to a halt in order to watch her.

As he plucked out her fancy filigree hair combs and bobby pins, her eyes closed. The weighty skein of her hair unfurled, and he very gently, very slowly went about unwinding and finger-combing the fine strands until they hung like a rippled golden cape around her shoulders. "Don't be afraid," he coaxed, because he had felt the tremors that coursed through her with each pass of his hand.

"I'm not afraid, exactly," she said breathlessly. Her lashes rose, then dipped shyly, revealing only a glint of blue. "I—I'm shivering with anticipation." A short huff of nervous, high-pitched laughter made her bite down hard on her lower lip. She winced in pain.

Holding her chin in his fingers, he shallowly dipped his thumb into her mouth, feeling her sharp intake of breath. He found her moist inner lip and used the wetness to soothe the bite mark, stroking her lip until it glistened provocatively. A throbbing need tightened his groin.

Puckering, Charlotte pressed a tiny kiss on the tip of his

thumb. When his fingers spread to caress her face, she rolled her cheek against his palm and kissed each of his fingertips in turn, making small sounds of pleading that were so erotic he felt as if he were bursting into flames.

They kissed deeply. Quinn filled his hands with her luxuriant hair and buried his face in it, inhaling its peachy, faintly spicy scent. "I want to feel your hair sliding through my fingers like silk," he said, watching the fine spun-gold strands fan from his fingertips like gossamer webbing.

Charlotte's eyes shone. "Oh, Quinn…"

With both hands he skimmed over the liquid satin of her loose top, stopping at the wide, black velvet hem. Despite her encouragement, he wasn't sure if he should go on, particularly when he remembered what he'd written in the second valentine. At the time, all this had been an unreachable fantasy.

She settled the matter by pulling the top off over her head. For a moment she clutched it to her bare abdomen in defense, gathering courage, then tossed the garment aside. She looked into his eyes, holding them even as he gradually realized that she wasn't wearing a bra, only the pearls, erotic against her luminous bare skin. The tight pink buds of her breasts peeked out at him from the scrim of her waist-length hair.

"See it draped golden over your bare breasts," he whispered, afraid to touch her until she gave a little cry and came into his arms of her own volition. And then he was touching her everywhere, electrified by the feel of her fine pale skin and silken hair, the weight of her breasts and the hard nubs of her nipples. The warm flush and frank eagerness of her response negated his fear that she would be a fragile china doll he'd handle clumsily. Although he suspected that Charlotte would always retain some of his original image of an ivory tower princess, he understood that she was also a vital, hungry, needy woman. A match for even his strongest appetites, whether or not she knew it yet herself.

Thankful for the ease of elastic waistbands, he pushed down her wide-legged pants, his caresses lingering upon the flare of her hips until she was swiveling them like a belly dancer. Impelled to continue the dance, he dropped to his knees before her, trailing kisses along the tempting curve of her belly. His palms stroked upward along the backs of her thighs. When he reached the plump swell of her backside and teasingly slid a fingertip along its crease, Charlotte gave a great shudder. Her knees buckled and she sagged against him, breathing hard, her fists clenched in his hair. "I don't think I can stand—"

"Shh," he said, holding her as he worked one-armed to discard the satin pants and spread her coat over a teak bench. "I'll take care of you." He lowered her to the bench, regretting that he hadn't planned for cushions.

Wide-eyed, silent, Charlotte brought her long bare legs against her torso and gripped them tightly. Still kneeling, Quinn kissed her knuckles. Her smile flickered like the candle flames. She was still unsure, but starting to relax. He stroked her crossed ankles until she uncrossed them with a sigh. He slipped off her tasseled flats and kissed the arch of her foot, the instep, the pink-polished nail of her big toe. Muffled giggles had begun to sneak past the hand she'd pressed to her mouth, so he took two of her toes into his mouth, his tongue teasingly exploring the hollow between them.

"Quinn!" she said, hiccuping with laughter as he continued to finger and suck on her toes. "Stop! That *tickles*...." By now she was reclining on her elbows, entirely at ease, her head thrown back, her stomach muscles clenching and her breasts jiggling enticingly.

"Say uncle." He ran his pointed tongue along the tops of her toes as if playing scales on a piano.

"Uncle!" She kicked playfully. "Oh. Stop. Please—thank you—whatever. *Uncle—!*"

No, thank *you*, Quinn thought, hammered by the shadowy glimpse of amber-colored curls and sweet pink flesh her kick had unwittingly allowed him. *Thank you very much.*

Suddenly the air in the greenhouse was as thick and warm as soup. Every cell in Quinn's body swelled expectantly in the lengthening silence. Charlotte's lips parted, but her question remained unspoken. *She knew.* She had to—one look at the tension in his face was all it took.

His erection was so painful it hurt to move, but slowly he smoothed his palms up her legs, reaching for the double loops of pearls. "Twine your pearls around my hands," he said hoarsely, his gut clenching as he did so, "and roll them…" With a low moan, Charlotte lay flat on the bench, arching her back as he languidly rolled the pearls over her breasts, pressing them into her flesh, rubbing them back and forth across her nipples. "…Over your naked, twisting body," he finished. She'd flung her arms over her head and was holding onto the bench like a lifeline while the rest of her body twisted sinuously, her feet flat on the bench and her knees raised, hips and torso alternately lifting as he stroked the pearls from her breasts to her belly and back again. He stopped to loop them around one of her breasts, decoratively encircling the prominent nipple until he leaned over to take it into his mouth, after which the rope of pearls was abandoned in the rapid rise of more urgent passions. She whimpered as he swirled his tongue and sucked hard, wanting to devour her engorged flesh, to take her into himself in some primal way.

When the urge became too much, he forced himself to sit back on his heels and just look at her. She was an extravagant work of art, the candlelight playing over the wet, pearlescent peaks and shadowed valleys of her body, laid out before him for a bacchanalian feast.

She turned her face toward his, her eyes glowing, her mouth curved into a gentle, giving smile that went straight to his heart. "Watch your eyes get bright," he said.

He kissed her lightly, sweetly. "Your lips go soft."

And skimmed his hand along her undulating body. "Your skin glow pink in the candlelight...."

"Yes," she whispered.

With savage efficiency, he stripped off his turtleneck, loathe to have her out of his sight for even one second. She sank her fingertips into the crisp brown hair that matted his chest and softly said, "Oh, yes," as he angled closer and took her mouth in a long, luscious kiss that tasted like spun sugar and mint and warm, willing woman.

When he broke away, they looked into each other's eyes and said together, in perfect sync: "Delectable."

Quinn rose and dropped his trousers and briefs, piercingly aware of Charlotte's big eyes as he lifted her legs and sank onto the bench, straddling it, his arousal hot and heavy and aching as he parted her thighs and deftly touched the dewy curls between them. She made a mewling sound, like a kitten. He touched her again, sliding one finger inside the tender petals of flesh, and heard the blood rushing in his ears as he lowered his head and kissed her there, exactly there, parting her with his fingers so her molten desire flowed over his tongue. And she moaned his name like an invocation, her hands on her breasts, her hips rising to meet the shocking pleasure of his intimate kiss.

He lifted his head, said thickly, "I want the taste of you in my mouth," and before she could think to turn shy, he slid forward, wrapped her legs around his waist and pressed himself into her, going slowly, so slowly it was painful, because he was strikingly aware of the necessity of subjugating his need to hers. She was tight, but liquid, clasping him in warmth as he entered her millimeter by millimeter. Even with his blood raging like a forest fire, every instinct roaring for him to take her now, hard and fast and deep, he tried to speak, grinding each difficult word between his gritted teeth. But all he could manage was a strangled, "Your—velvet—warmth—" before the savage need overtook him and he lost the last of his restraints.

DEEP INSIDE!

A split second before she voiced it, Charlotte felt the scream rising inside her. It was a scream of ecstasy, of passion, but Quinn might not realize that, and with an effort she withheld most of it, letting out only a long, shrill, keening sound that rose in the warm greenhouse like the distant howl of a wolf.

Quinn shuddered over her, his arms braced on the bench, gone so rigid with tension every sinew, tendon and vein stood out in harsh relief. "Are you okay?" He shifted and pressed one hand to the small of her back, lifting her off the bench and into his lap. They slid together and clung, interlocked. "Did I hurt you?"

She shook her head, even though that wasn't strictly true. His last, hard thrust had been excruciating, but exquisite. She felt pierced, rent, turned inside out. Forever changed. And when she glanced down to where they were joined—!

Charlotte squeezed her thighs around Quinn's waist, eliciting a gravel-rough moan that made her shiver inside and out. He was so thick, so hard, so *deep* inside her that she couldn't bring herself to meet his searching gaze. The intimacy was too much. Instead she twined herself around him, pressing her face into his shoulder. His skin was smooth, slick, salty, the wide bands of his muscles hard as iron under her hands. The thick pelt on his chest scraped her breasts when she sucked in another shaky breath, the pearls pressed round and warm between them. The ridged muscles in his stomach were taut against her belly as he held himself still, waiting for her.

Waiting deep inside her.

Tentatively Charlotte rocked her hips. Even the smallest movement was explosive, like sparklers under her skin. She twisted against Quinn, corkscrewing the pleasure and sweet pain into a tight hot spiral that lit her up inside. Shuddering, he pressed deeper, one hand on her hip, the other molding her breast against his chest, his callused thumb and forefinger squeezing and rotating the nipple. And she wound even tighter.

With her elbows resting on his wide shoulders, she cradled his head in her hands and kissed the fringe of his shorn hair, his creased brow, his closed eyelids. She felt them quiver under her lips, his eyes rolling back as the strain became too much. He growled like an animal and plunged his hips against hers, deep and fast and continuous, the wrenching force of it leaving her breathless and weak. But Quinn pressed her thighs open and slid his hands beneath her bottom and lifted her into the burning, twisting, driving rhythm until something inside her gave way and the hot spiral flew apart into what seemed like a million glittering pieces, all of them swallowed by the white-hot vortex of agony and ecstasy, ecstasy and agony, forever one and the same.

QUINN WAS ALL she'd ever dreamed of, Charlotte thought lazily, watching as he slipped into his trousers and went over to the table and opened the champagne. She pulled the coat around herself, shivering, but not from cold. The greenhouse was practically a steam bath, the glass dripping with a thick condensation, the air heavy with warmth and the perfume of sweet flora and earthy loam. She was utterly content.

Except for one thing.

Where did they go from here?

Quinn hadn't given her a clue about his intentions after tonight. The valentines had led only to this moment, not beyond. And as much as she tried to tell herself that she could be satisfied with one magical evening, Charlotte knew that wasn't so. She'd fallen in love with her black velvet prince. She wanted a happily-ever-after.

Restlessly she slipped on her shoes and went outside, to her usual place in the turret. The night air was shockingly cold. It should have cleared her head of any yearning, sentimental, romantic notions, but it didn't.

Breaking long habit, she pressed her back against the curved turret wall and stared at the greenhouse instead of the view. It glowed with wavering candlelight. Quinn's silhouette moved among the shadows cast against the misted glass by the palms and other greenery. When finally he came outside to join her, Charlotte's heart turned over. She swallowed hard and turned her face up to the heavens. *Please let him want me as much as I want him,* she prayed to the milky blue-black sky. It didn't seem too much to ask.

"You forgot something," Quinn said huskily, looming over her in the dark in his black clothes and new face. He hesitated for a moment, then said, "Me."

She released her breath. "Oh, Quinn, I can't imagine ever forgetting you. Even if..." *Even if you left me.* "Even after a thousand years."

He pressed a glass of champagne into her hand and touched his own to it with a soft, crystalline clink. "To the millennium, then."

She wouldn't drink. "To a shared millennium," she

said bravely, letting the implied question hover between them.

Quinn cleared his throat. "Maybe it's time you opened the final valentine." He pulled it from his pocket and handed it to her, the tops of his ears gone pink in the lights from Fifth Avenue.

Charlotte held the envelope between her palms, her chin tipped up, her heart in her throat. For all her concern, one look at Quinn's face was all the assurance she needed. Oh, yes, she *knew*. His conviction was as palpable as the stone wall at her back, the emotion in his eyes unmistakable. How could she have ever questioned his devotion when he had already answered her dreams?

Excited now, she tore open the envelope and removed the card. Snowflakes had begun to fall from the dark sky; they drifted onto the valentine, their patterns as intricate as those of the lacy hearts. Smiling, Charlotte brushed the black velvet across her cheek, her lips, vowing that she would never doubt herself or Quinn again.

At last she opened the card and read the inscription. *Together forever, my valentine.*

She looked up at Quinn with stars in her eyes. "Together forever?" she whispered.

He put their champagne glasses on the tower wall and took her face in his hands and kissed the snowflakes from her hair and cheeks and lips. "My valentine."

Charlotte laughed and snuggled into him, feeling as happy and free and full of love as the most innocent child in the world. "Oh, look," she said, her eye caught by a movement on the street below, "there's Hattie and Everett." She hung over the wall, waving like a little kid, her golden hair blowing in the swirling snow. "*Hallooo*, Hattie." The housekeeper and the dry cleaner were walking along the street, holding hands, bundled in winter coats, boots and scarves. They turned up their faces, blinking at the snow, and waved. Hattie's broad grin could have been seen from the moon.

Quinn twined his arms around Charlotte from behind and tugged on her lapels. "Careful. You're almost spilling out of that."

Although she'd forgotten that she was still nude beneath her coat, Quinn's arms were wrapped around her, keeping her safe and snug and decent. They stood leaning against the turret wall for a long while, not talking, not needing to, just enjoying the brisk night and the thickening snow and the warmth of knowing they belonged to each other.

Charlotte's lips moved in a silent promise.

Together forever, my valentine.

Two Hearts

A full moon, a hot tub, Valentine's Day and a love potion—a potent combination.
As are the twin brothers who succumb to the seduction. With shocking results...!

Love for sale

PANSY KINGSMITH might have passed the nondescript storefront a hundred times before she noticed the small placard leaning in its frosty window. In elegant calligraphy, complete with excessive swoops and swirls and tiny spider-shaped ink blots, the sign read:

Potions   Charms   Philtres
"Good Valentine, be kind to me,
In dreams let me my true love see."

And below that, scrawled in red marker:

20% Off Pre-Valentine's Day Sale

Despite the frivolity inherent in Pansy's given name—and how she wished it had been given to someone else!—she had painstakingly trained herself to be a sensible woman, one not prone to whimsy. She walked on despite the intriguing possibilities invoked by the placard, going slowly only because the sidewalk was slippery with snow and ice.

After six careful steps, she paused to hitch up the strap of her book bag. She wiggled her fingers inside her mittens; her breath puffed in the cold air. *Potions, Charms, Philtres. "Good Valentine, be kind to me...."* She frowned. What complete nonsense.

Pansy trudged by Copy Copy. She passed Le Junque and the old-fashioned, tan brick five-and-dime. She got as far as the heap of plowed snow near the corner of Nitschke Street before she stopped. The image of Jesse Angelini's handsome face had forced itself into her mind and refused to be shooed away.

She gave herself up to a sigh of longing. If there really *were* such things as love potions, Jesse was the man she'd use one on.

When Jesse Angelini—ex-jock turned successful sportscaster, hunk extraordinaire and playboy without peer—had moved in next door, Pansy tried to be sensible about her chances. Jesse attracted women like a magnet, women of every type and personality. From high-heeled beauty queens to savvy businesswomen to bouncy college cheerleaders, they all had one thing in common: they were gorgeous. As a merely pretty, pleasingly plump nature book editor, Pansy felt she couldn't compete. Nor did she care to.

Nonetheless, once Jesse had gotten around to noticing her, she'd fallen hard for him on their very first date, despite her cautious nature. By the second date she was firmly in love and busily convincing herself that their relationship would be different than his others because she was a different type of woman.

How Jesse had remained oblivious to her feelings was a mystery. Perhaps he hadn't—their third date had ended on her doorstep with Jesse saying in a sincere, concerned, gentlemanly way that she was a wonderful person and a whole lot of fun, but he was a footloose bachelor and as they were next-door neighbors it might be best if they stayed friends, just friends, and she was a real pal to agree. *A real pal!*

Stricken speechless at the decimation of all her mounting hopes, Pansy had managed only a nod, stifling a whimper as injured pride forced her to suffer Jesse's ignominious kiss-off kiss. On the forehead.

And that was that—as far as Jesse was concerned. Pansy had found it impossible to rein in her emotions so easily. Regardless of Jesse's quickly reassumed parade of conquests, she continued to believe that one day he'd appreciate what she offered: stability, devotion, loyalty, a happy family life complete with adorable children and a supportive, modestly accomplished wife who loved him with all her heart.

Pansy had the will to make the relationship work. What she needed was something to get it jump-started....

Slowly she turned back the way she'd come, reluctant feet dragging her past the five-and-dime and the resale furniture shop and the copy store. Perhaps she was silly to take the sign seriously, but why not just this once give in to impulse? What harm could it do?

She thought of her ditsy mother, talking baby talk to her plants and sprinkling rose water over her crystals. She thought of her scatterbrained father, searching his fusty office for the book that was in his hand or the glasses that were perched on the top of his head. They were nice people, and Pansy loved them, but they wafted from one catastrophe to another—*Who forgot to file the income tax return? A saw-your-own skylight—why not? Hey, let's cash in our retirement fund for tickets to Egypt!*—oblivious to their daughter's exasperation. All her life, Pansy had denied her own inclination toward similar dipsy-doodle tendencies.

Still, that was no reason—or not much of one—why she couldn't take a glance around the love potion shop to see if its merchandise was all the placard promised. Just this one time. Just out of curiosity. She didn't have to actually *buy* anything.

Then again, a twenty-percent-off sale was nothing to snicker at.

Pansy stopped in front of the store. The small sign had vanished from the window. Taken aback, she first wondered if Jesse had done such a number on her that she'd conjured up the malarkey about love potions out of wishful thinking. But then she reminded herself that she did not indulge in flights of fancy. Besides, the frost-rimed, leaded-glass window still displayed a row of tall vials and cut-glass decanters with bunches of herbs suspended in jewel-colored liquids. It was only the sign that was missing.

Pansy studied the glass containers. Oils? she wondered. Unguents…tinctures…aphrodisiacs?

Aphrodisiacs! The very word gave her an instinctive thrill. Immediately she imagined Jesse, handsome Jesse and his fabulous, nearly naked body, beckoning to her from the cloud of steam that was perpetually billowing off the hot tub in his sunroom. Jesse—Jesse wanting *her*, only her, his blue eyes gleaming with wicked intent, his broad, bronze, muscular chest gleaming with moisture, his perfect white teeth just plain gleaming…

The snowplow roared by, breaking into Pansy's steamy little fantasy. Despite the twenty-degree weather, she was suddenly very warm inside her down-filled parka. And that was just…preposterous. She was dropping her standards right and left.

As Pansy unwound her scarf, peeled off her mittens and shoved them into her pockets, she told herself to remain sensible. The bottles in the window likely held something entirely innocuous—like vinegar salad dressing. *Potions, charms and philtres, indeed!*

It was odd, though, that she hadn't noticed this shop before, especially as it obviously wasn't new. Belle Terre, Wisconsin, with a population that reached the fifteen thousand mark only if you counted pets, was not exactly an anonymous, overcrowded city. By all rights, the "love potion" store should have attracted a good deal of notice among Belle Terre's curious, chatty citizenry.

Cautiously, Pansy gauged the situation. The shop shared walls with the businesses on either side, tucked between their prosperous-looking exteriors like a sparrow's egg nestled in a bright Easter basket. The cracked, gray cedar shingles were dull beside Copy Copy's crisp white siding and orange trim. The panes of the small display window were spangled with ice crystals, rubbed clear only in the center of each. Pansy cupped her hands around her eyes and peered inside, but what with the dim interior and her breath fogging the glass, all that she could make out was an open wooden crate spewing excelsior, and a bank of cluttered shelves layered with dust.

She was a fastidious person; only the prospect of snaring Jesse Angelini, however far-fetched, could have lured her into what looked to be a rather dingy and unorganized store.

The solid oak plank door was old enough to have rounded, smooth edges. A stained-glass inset depicted an open treasure chest overflowing with amber glass "coins." The brass latch was heavy and carved with unusual designs, but it was strangely warm beneath her bare hand, considering that the air was so cold. Someone must have just touched it, she thought...with a steam iron. Or perhaps they'd finally invented a self-warming doorknob.

She glanced up and down Nitschke Street. It was quiet in the dull gray winter light. Eerily so. With all the other businesses closed since 5:00 or 6:00 p.m., there was not a soul in sight.

Touched by an apprehension she didn't understand and thus chose to ignore, Pansy quickly opened the door and stepped inside. She jerked her hand away as if the brass handle was a living thing. *It was*, her instincts screamed. *No, it wasn't*, her rational mind said. She stared

at her palm for a moment, then at the door, telling herself
that any momentary sensations of the warm brass latch
moving within her grip were simply impossible!

She made a fist. Even as her educated self reassuringly
recited the properties of matter, a knot of worry burst
from the more instinctive regions, sending tiny shards of
fear prickling through her bloodstream. Pansy Kingsmith
did not appreciate what she could not readily define.

Defiant, she took a deep breath and threw off her hood.
And sneezed explosively.

Dust was everywhere, and clutter, and heaps of rough
wooden crates opened to display their jumbled contents.
There may have even been cobwebs in the corners, but
Pansy was too dismayed by what she saw around her to
inspect that far. Snuffling, she held out the sleeve of one of
the limp, tattered garments hung on a circular rack,
pinching the yellowed lace between the tips of two fingers, half expecting a moth to flutter out. A black velvet
cape hemmed in fake ermine slipped from a hanger and
came to rest on the floorboards.

Halloween costumes? Pansy shook her head. What sort
of weird place was this? She pressed a finger under her
nose and advanced into the gloom, trying not to disturb
any more of the dust. A pink feather boa foamed from an
open carton. Dark, scary tribal masks hung high on the
walls. A glass case with a cracked top was filled with unusual jewelry—heavy, baroque pieces dripping with
gems set side by side with strings of wooden beads and
wide metal bracelets. Cuffs, really. Pansy rubbed at the
smeared glass with a mitten. Did the pair of hammered
copper cuffs actually come equipped with a lock and key?

"Oh, my," she whispered.

A wall of narrow, partitioned shelves above the main
counter caught her notice. Innumerable containers of
every color and shape filled its cubbyholes. Stone mortars
and pestles, glass vials, minuscule flasks with dulled in-

scriptions. Round clay pots stoppered with cork, mesh bags filled with bay leaves, braided wands of lavender, scrolls of birch bark tied with raffia. And, bubbling ominously on a bright red coil behind the counter, a pot of something green, glutinous and so strongly pungent it nearly blotted out the shop's more pleasant aroma of lavender, patchouli and verbena. Pansy pinched her nostrils.

"Hello?" she called nasally, then released her nose and lifted her voice. "Anyone here?"

There was no answer. Just silence as thick as the dust.

Pansy drew herself up distastefully. What was she, of all people, doing in such a place? *Leave at once*, she told her feet, scowling down at her boots when they refused to obey. Unzipping her parka instead, she eyed a row of barrels and boxes lined up along the front of the counter. Her nose wrinkled.

Bulbous, gnarled, rootlike things, hairy with spidery tendrils, filled one of the barrels. *Mandrake*, she thought, pulling the name out of nowhere. *Gross*. She edged away, feeling like Alice, having stepped through the looking glass into an existence the total opposite of her safe, sane little world.

The world of a woman so ordinary and unexciting she couldn't blame Jesse Angelini for dropping her.

The thought halted Pansy's retreat. "Hello?" she called once more. "Are you open for business?"

Still no answer. She wanted to leave, but she couldn't. Cockeyed hopefulness gripped her. *If there is any chance at all, I must take it*, she vowed. Once she'd enticed Jesse to give her a closer look, he would see that she was what he didn't know he wanted. There was no reason why they couldn't make a very successful couple.

The sound of shuffling footsteps came from the back room, signaling the shopkeeper's approach at last. A stout, middle-aged woman parted a beaded curtain behind the counter, beringed fingers splayed out before her to lead the way. "Ah, a customer," she said, her voice rich with an exotic Eastern European accent. "A rare customer, Aphrodite. We must make her welcome."

The shopkeeper's flowing, multicolored caftan and black velvet turban held Pansy's notice until she realized the woman had spoken to the black-and-white bird perched on her shoulder. The bird tilted its head and seemed to regard Pansy thoughtfully. Its round black eyes looked like jellied currants—strangely intelligent jellied currants.

Pansy felt certain that the bird was reading her mind. She tried to scorn the notion as something her mother might invent. Apparently the shop's otherworldly atmosphere was affecting her perceptions; she normally didn't believe in the anthropomorphism of animals. Even Tux, her own cat, an exceptionally regal creature with a neat white bib and sleek black coat, was only a cat—not a bridegroom.

"My name is Mademoiselle Grimaldi," announced the shopkeeper. She had sallow skin beneath heavy makeup that further emphasized the exotic qualities of her dark, arched brows, hooded eyes and strongly Roman nose.

With a sudden flutter and flap, the bird flew from her shoulder to a perch in one of the cobwebby corners. "And that was my magpie, Aphrodite Urania, named after the goddess of wedded love." The woman waggled a finger. "Not Aphrodite Pandemos, goddess of free love. Oh, no, no, certainly not!"

Pansy had ducked when the bird swooped by; now she straightened, brushing back her short auburn curls. "Er, I'm...I..." At a loss, she could only shrug, her palms upturned. "I'm not sure why I'm here."

Mademoiselle Grimaldi reached across the counter to snatch one of Pansy's hands out of the air. "We shall soon know."

Pansy let out a squeak of surprise, but allowed herself to be drawn closer. "What are you doing—"

"Hush." The shopkeeper pursed her lips and leaned over Pansy's right palm, holding it lightly in her warm, soft hand, tracing the tips of her scarlet nails over the lines, rubbing the pad of her thumb over the fleshy mound at the base of Pansy's.

Pansy shivered despite herself. Palm reading was pure balderdash—something her mother indulged in over the kitchen table with her astrologer friend, Fatima Kowalski, when they'd tired of tea leaves and tarot cards. It was not for sensible, straight-thinking people like Pansy.

"You seek great love, lasting love." Mademoiselle Grimaldi batted her thick false lashes and added coyly, "*Physical* love." She pursed lips painted as bright as blood oranges and released Pansy's hand with a reassuring pat. "Mademoiselle sees angel in your future. By Valentine's Day."

Angel? Pansy's heart skipped a beat. She folded her fingers against the lingering, preternatural warmth of her palm, thinking of Jesse's surname—Angelini—as she pressed the fist to her chest. Could it be?

Then she remembered herself and drew back. This was how pseudopsychics roped in their marks, by luring them into supplying their own interpretation of what was no more than a shot in the dark. "I can't imagine who," she said stiffly.

"Angel," the magpie chirped, making Pansy flinch. She cast it a wild glance.

"There was a sign in the window," she blurted. "Now it's gone." The charms, potions and philtres part was what had interested her. Instead, like a good little bargain hunter, she said, "Twenty percent off for Valentine's Day?"

The shopkeeper was stirring the stinking glutinous

mass in the pot. "Aha, you saw sign." She nodded knowingly. "We suspect as much."

"Why did you remove it?"

The woman's smile was inscrutable. "Did we?" The bird cackled and danced on its perch. Mademoiselle Grimaldi turned back to the pot, muttering a brief incantation beneath her breath as she spooned the gluey green soup into a cluster of small jars.

We? Pansy's glance darted toward the bird, which was now arching its neck and fluffing its feathers, looming in the corner like Poe's raven or one of Stephen King's menacing crows. Its eyes glittered at her, making her nape prickle ominously. She stood her ground. "Might I ask what you're making?"

"Ach, one of my special recipes. Smidgen of this, noggin of that. Not right for your purposes, Pansy, my dear."

"I shouldn't think so." Pansy sniffed; the smell was still repulsive. "But…how did you know my name?"

"Ahh, yes. Pansy—a sweet, romantic flower. Also known as heartsease and love-in-idleness." Mademoiselle Grimaldi gestured eloquently, her plump fingers carving the air, the stones in her rings glowing in the dim light. "Pity the poor pansy—stricken by Cupid's arrow, bled purple with love's wound."

Pansy didn't like the sound of that. "How did you know?" she repeated firmly.

"Mademoiselle Grimaldi has a small talent," the woman said, inclining her head modestly. But the accompanying mischievous wink of one kohl-lined eye led Pansy to believe that she was being played like a fish. She supposed that one would have to pull out all the theatrics to reel in one's catch if one was purporting to sell potions, charms and philtres. It would do her well to remember that this was entertainment, not reality.

Still…

"You sell—" Pansy lowered her voice "—love potions?" She paused. "*Aphrodisiacs?*"

Mademoiselle Grimaldi nodded. "To those who believe."

Pansy tried to be skeptical. "In what?"

The inscrutable smile reappeared. "In love, of course."

Well, that was easy enough. Pansy believed in love—it was the *potion* part she was having trouble with.

"Love is most powerful of forces," intoned the shopkeeper. "The heart can be, shall we say, headstrong." She propped her fingers in a steeple and engaged Pansy's eyes. "Often difficult to contain."

Pansy knew that. The rush of feelings she experienced every time she ran into Jesse was almost impossible to conceal, and still she timed her comings and goings to coincide with his. Which could be why lately he seemed to be avoiding her.

"Mademoiselle Grimaldi must be very careful, very respectful of great talent. All potions are chosen wisely, as are recipients." The shopkeeper looked Pansy up and down. "But you—you are already certain of heart's desire, no?"

"I—I...yes, I am."

"Angel," squawked the magpie.

"Mademoiselle Grimaldi has just the thing." The shopkeeper sailed toward the back room, her rainbow-striped caftan floating in her wake.

Pansy tried to withdraw, at least mentally. Although even to the skeptical mind there seemed to be a sense of mystery and magic—*black* magic, perhaps—in the air, she was no longer certain that she wanted to fool with the natural progress of love. Then again, as she didn't truly believe in this junk despite Mademoiselle Grimaldi's sales pitch, it would do no harm to try one. It could be that a "love potion" would provide her with the extra bit of confidence that would make her more attractive to Jesse.

These things were often a question of positive thinking rather than magic.

Mademoiselle Grimaldi returned, holding aloft a tall, slender, gently curved glass vial filled with a pale apricot fluid. "Angel Water," she said portentously. "Prophetic, no?"

Pansy struggled to retain her skepticism. Deep inside, she wanted to believe. She ached to believe. Which was merely the assertion of her mother's bad influence, she decided, and said doubtfully, "It looks like colored water."

Mademoiselle Grimaldi clucked her tongue. "Powerful love philtre. An aphrodisiac, my dear."

Mmm, the dark, erotic wonders of aphrodisia...

Pansy managed to catch herself before she could lapse into another fantasy about Jesse gone crazy with passion for her just in time for Valentine's Day. The sheer absurdity of that happening made her respond acerbically. "Tell me it's not toxic. If I water my plants with it, will they wither and die? If my cat drinks some accidentally will he fall in love with me, too?"

The shopkeeper's dimpled chin snapped up; her fleshy second chin wobbled with outrage. "Perhaps Mademoiselle Grimaldi has been wrong about you. Perhaps you do not fully appreciate the power of love."

Hastily, Pansy relented. "Oh, no, please—I'll take it. I only want to be certain it's not dangerous."

Mademoiselle Grimaldi offered another crafty smile. "There is danger and there is danger, little Pansy. You shall be instructed on proper usage, and if you do exactly as Mademoiselle says..." She shrugged. "Safe as houses."

Pansy swallowed dryly. "Can't you tell me what's in this...Angel Water?"

Instead of answering, the woman tossed the fringed tail of her purple scarf over one shoulder and opened the glass display case. She reached for a basket of polished stones and began to finger through them, lingering over the striped agates.

Except for the click of the shiny stones, the shop was ominously silent. Its mystical aura wrapped around Pansy's doubts like a thick blanket, lulling her skepticism. Gradually she realized she couldn't hear a sound from the street, not the thrum of a car engine nor the shout of a child. The reasonable explanation was that Nitschke Street was not heavily traversed and the shop's plank door was solid enough to shut out what traffic sounds there were. No need to see deep, dark meaning where there was none....

Mademoiselle Grimaldi made a selection. She slipped the stone into a tiny black velvet bag, knotted the drawstrings and slid it across the counter. "What do I do with this?" asked Pansy, poking tentatively at the velvet pouch.

"Angel Water is love philtre. Once your intended has bathed in it on the night of the full moon he will be bound to you for lifetime. Use all at once, every drop—you must not hold back or enchantment will be weakened." Mademoiselle Grimaldi went on to list further instructions and cautions: Pansy was not to bathe in the stuff herself or the philtre's staying power would be diluted; sharing the potion was not advised; the proprietor was not liable for the consequences of misguided applications. "The agate is simple love token," she concluded. "Place in toe of shoe and it will bring him to you."

"Will this really work?" Pansy found herself whispering, the velvet pouch pressed between her palms. Suddenly she believed. She believed with all her heart.

Mademoiselle made another of her elaborate gestures, like an artist painting arabesques in the air. "If hearts are in accord, yes, it will work."

"Angel," chirped the magpie. "Angel, angel, angel."

2

Back to earth

PANSY'S ACQUIRED skepticism had returned by the time she reached her home on Adderley Avenue. Still, one look next door at Jesse Angelini's tall, mansard-roofed Victorian and the longing in her heart renewed itself. She'd admired the house even before Jesse had moved in. It was so easy to imagine herself living there, planting the window boxes with red geraniums in the spring, hoisting a flag from the porch on the Fourth of July, lighting the fire, roasting a turkey, laughing at her husband as he wrangled a twelve-foot Christmas tree up the front steps....

She cradled the book bag's fragile cargo to her chest and reached into her mailbox, still surveying Jesse's house from pineapple finial to herringbone brick walk. He wouldn't be home yet from the Green Bay TV station where he worked. Staying late at the office and then stopping to buy the love potion had meant she'd missed Jesse's six o'clock sportscast for the first time in weeks.

Pansy stuffed her mail into the book bag, pausing to run her fingertips over the frosted-glass bottle tucked inside to be sure that it had made the trip home safely. Satisfied, she rang her landlord's doorbell. Quentin Barney, a retired widower, lived on the first two floors of his plain green frame house. Pansy rented the attic, a large square room with a window in each of four dormers, and a balcony that overlooked the backyard.

Though she frequently dropped in for casual visits with Mr. Barney, this evening's agenda included an ulterior motive. Her landlord had the most thorough set of encyclopedias she'd ever seen, inside a library or out, and a matching mind for esoteric detail.

The door opened and Mr. Barney, tall, pear shaped, bald and kind, peered out. "Pansy! You're late this evening, aren't you? The WKSS newscast was over twenty minutes ago. Not much cooking in sports. Jesse's top story was something about when the Brewers' pitchers will report for spring training."

Pansy winced. Was her crush on Jesse as obvious as all that?

The landlord opened the door wider. "Come inside where it's warm, Pansy. Let me take your bag—lots of manuscripts, have we?"

"I've got it, thanks." She felt protective of the love potion, even though it was probably just a bottle of colored water. "I brought an advance copy of *Songbirds of the Upper Midwest: Revised for the Twenty-first Century*." Mr. Barney was a backyard bird-watcher; when he'd found out she was a book editor at NatureWords, a small regional press, her three-year lease had been clinched on the spot.

Once inside, she shed her winter gear and sat on the fringed, ruby velvet hassock beside Mr. Barney's favorite overstuffed armchair. She hugged her knees, taking a moment to bask in the warmth of the dark, cloistered, fire-lit room before she unzipped the book bag. Shielding the slender neck of the corked bottle, she pulled out a reader's copy of one of NatureWords's spring releases and handed it to her landlord, knowing what would happen.

"My, my, this looks good," he said with relish, settling the earpieces of his reading glasses in place. He turned on the standing Tiffany-style lamp, squirmed into his chair's well-developed divot and opened to the first page. Within a minute he was thoroughly absorbed, shoulders stooped, index finger running along the lines of print, softly whistling bird calls under his breath.

Pansy set down her bag and went to the glass-doored cherry bookcases that flanked the fireplace. Mr. Barney allowed her free access to his encyclopedias, but under normal circumstances he'd have been hovering at her shoulder, spouting odd facts, eager to help her with whatever she wanted to look up. The love potion was one thing she intended to keep to herself; she didn't care to appear as foolish and gullible as she already felt.

The first volume went up to only the mid *A*'s, so she took down the second and flipped through the pages until she came to *Aphrodisiacs*. She skimmed a lengthy history, and found a cross-reference to Angel Water. "See Angel Water," she murmured, and paged through the list of aphrodisiacs. The entry was short, but there was a recipe.

Angel Water was a blend of orange flower water, rose water, myrtle water, distilled spirit of musk and spirit of ambergris. Nothing more.

Despite herself, Pansy was disappointed. Angel Water wasn't magical. It wasn't even all that exotic. She'd heard of ambergris, but took out Volume I to look it up nonetheless: a waxy substance produced by sperm whales, once thought to be an aphrodisiac, now used mainly to make perfume.

Sperm whales. *Lovely.*

Pansy reconsidered the whole love potion scheme. Mademoiselle Grimaldi had stressed that Pansy must follow the instructions to the letter, but, really, how was she to do that? There was no legitimate way to invite herself into Jesse's bathroom. If she simply gave him the vial and said it was bath oil, would he use it—and on the night of the full moon? Say he did, and was actually overcome with passion for her? What would she do then?

Well…if her fantasies were any indication, she'd break

out the satin sheets and do the horizontal mambo with him until the spell wore off. And then when the sun came up she'd lay in a lifetime supply of Angel Water and start planning the wedding.

Pansy blinked. Oh, for Pete's sake! Despite all her years of denial, one sniff of Valentine's Day hocus-pocus and she'd reverted to her true colors as a naive and hopeless and apparently *horny* romantic. Drat her mother for breeding such unruly tendencies into her!

Pansy heaved a sigh as heavy as a hay bale. The really rotten thing of it was that lovesick suitors with hot tubs just didn't appear on the doorstep of responsible drudges like herself—whether or not love potions were involved. Even if she lost her head and completely succumbed to her wildest dreams and far-fetched fancies, in the end "Cinderella" would still be just a fairy tale.

"Nuts," Pansy said under her breath.

Mr. Barney looked up. "This will cheer you up," he said, and pursed his lips. The burbling call of some obscure songbird filled the warm room, as real as if a flock had settled onto the sofa cushions and were singing their hearts out. It was very nice, but Pansy was more in the mood for "Jesse's Girl." Even "That Old Black Magic" would do.

Fantasy, she thought. *Magic, romance.* Aw, heck. Who needed it?

"Sounds great, Mr. Barney." She slipped Volumes I and II back in place and closed the bookshelf door. "I guess I'll be leaving now. Enjoy the book—it'll be published in a few months and I can probably cadge you a free copy." Dispiritedly she pulled the strap of the book bag over her shoulder.

"As always, you've done a superb job of editing," Mr. Barney said. "Thanks for the sneak preview, Pansy. You're a real sweetheart."

Sweetheart. Pansy kissed her landlord's cheek, but she

couldn't help cringing inside. Why was it only bookish, elderly ornithologists who thought so well of her? Why never athletic, square-jawed bachelors in the prime of life?

She paused near the door, moodily reflecting on the shop, Mademoiselle Grimaldi, her potions and philtres and beady-eyed bird. "Er, Mr. Barney? What do you know about magpies?"

"Magpies?" He cocked his head. "I believe they're a member of *Pica*, in the genus of the crow family, black-and-white, long tail."

"They talk?"

"Magpies are chatterboxes in their own right, but they don't imitate human speech, as such. You may be thinking of the mynah."

"No, I'm certain the owner said it was a magpie."

Mr. Barney hefted himself out the sagging armchair. "Let's look up both birds in my handy encyclopedia. Volume XXXII, if I'm not mistaken."

"Oh, no, Mr. Barney. That's all right. It was only a thought. I have to get home...." Pansy talked herself out the door, waving off her landlord's entreaties. Once Mr. Barney began delving into the encyclopedia she could wind up stuck in his living room all evening, and tonight she needed privacy in order to think things through.

Because tomorrow was the full moon. On the walk home, she'd looked it up on her wildflower-of-the-month pocket calendar.

Pansy glanced again at Jesse's house as she ascended the steep outside stairway to her attic apartment. Still dark. There were nights—quite a few, actually—when Jesse didn't come home at all after his six o'clock show. It wasn't that Pansy was a hopeless busybody with no life of her own; several of her windows and even her tiny balcony simply happened to have excellent views of his house. And since she was up so high, she had a bird's-eye vantage point of Jesse Angelini's comings and goings.

It wasn't like she was obsessed or anything.

Only slightly lovesick. And a lot love starved.

The love potion clinked in the book bag as she took out her door key. She felt reassured, even though she told herself that she still hadn't decided if she was desperate enough to grasp at the chance-in-a-million it offered.

Ten o'clock, Pansy's studio apartment

THIS WAS WAY BETTER than *Northern Exposure* reruns—even the seminaked-running-of-the-bulls episode!

Disbelieving her eyes, Pansy hopped up, sending pillows and unedited manuscript pages flying. Tux gave a grumbly yowl and sank his claws into the seat cushion of the wing chair, loathe to be disturbed from his perpetual nap. Pansy scurried around the attic apartment, trying to remember where she'd put the binoculars Mr. Barney had given her for Christmas. Naturally, he'd intended them for bird-watching. Even though black-capped chickadees were sort of cute, Pansy preferred Jesse Angelini. Particularly when he was right next door and getting as naked as the proverbial jaybird while she wasted time looking for—aha! She plucked the binoculars off a shelf and was back at the window before the books they'd been holding up toppled sideways.

"Scoot over, Tux." The cat rumbled and flopped over onto his side. Pansy knelt backward on the wing chair, supporting the binoculars on the high backrest while she separated the slats of the venetian blinds. She'd peeked out a minute ago to see if Jesse had gotten home yet and had been rewarded with an eyeful.

The glass sunroom addition at the back of the brick Victorian was lit up like a Broadway stage. While Pansy had long suspected that the indoor hot tub was the scene for

Jesse's frolics with his stream of accommodating ladies, she'd never wanted to confirm it. Certainly not with binoculars.

But this time he was alone.

And, just possibly, *naked*.

With a twist the glasses came into focus. The sunroom appeared plain as day, golden yellow in the night, though already the windows were getting foggy from the heat. Pansy could see only a section of the hot tub because of a big, spiky potted palm inside and the lattice on the snowy deck outside. But she saw enough to make her pulse race like a Triple Crown Thoroughbred.

"Oh, Jesse," she breathed. "Oh, wow, Jesse."

In dreams let me my true love see…!

Tux meowed loudly and started sharpening his claws on the fleece of Pansy's baggy sweats. She scarcely noticed the needle pricks of the cat's claws because all of her senses were trained on the man next door. He appeared to be wearing nothing but a robe. She was sure even that would be coming off.

Pansy lowered the binoculars. She probably shouldn't be doing this.

Then again, there he was. In all his glory. It would take more willpower than hers to ignore that fact. And it was practically his own fault for strutting his stuff in plain view.

"Make that plain binocular view," she muttered, putting her eyes to the glasses with only a faintly guilty conscience. Even good girls could occasionally be bad.

The glass walls of the sunroom glistened with melting snow, but she could still make out Jesse's shape quite clearly in between the wavy runnels and glinting droplets. The robe was navy blue, loosely tied around his waist. Yawning, he passed a hand over his hair, leaving it standing on end. Hmm. The rumpled look. Something different for Jesse at this hour, but she liked it. It was endearing.

When he leaned over to test the water she got a glimpse of his face before he turned his back. Even though he was as handsome as ever, she thought he looked a little tired. Maybe he was getting fed up with the playboy life-style. Maybe he was ready for something new. Tenderness swelled within her. "Aww," she sighed, wanting to take care of him.

Then he dropped the robe and he wasn't wearing trunks. Pansy blinked rapidly. *He was not wearing trunks,* and as he stood there in all his naked glory she knew she *really* wanted to take care of him.

He was beautiful. His body was—

Pansy made a funny sound in her throat, a cross between a squeak and a breathy gulp. Jesse's body was awesome. Not the way kids used the word, but awesome in a devastating way that made a grown woman sweat between her toes, itch in places she'd never be able to soothe on her own, and lose hold of every thought in her head so that she forgot even her own name.

Some sort of flower. Petunia? Daisy? Honeysuckle?

She sharpened the focus of the glasses and was glad to discover that not even Jesse was perfect. Pretty close to it, though. His realness saved him from calendar-boy perfection. There was a small red birthmark on his back, below his left shoulder blade—these binoculars were *powerful*. Also a scar on his elbow, and a certain stiffness about the way he moved toward the hot tub. Overall, he was in great shape. Muscular, not bulky; trim, yet not so lean she'd feel like a butterball beside him; extremely fit, but not to the point where she'd be compelled to bounce quarters off his abs. The tone of his skin was delicious—a light, natural tan so unlike her own dead-of-winter pallor that she *did* feel an odd compulsion to lick his bones clean.

She smacked her lips. Just call her Honeysuckle.

Hey. Wait a minute. Hadn't she previously noticed that Jesse managed to keep a deep bronze tan—deeper than what she was seeing now—even in February? She frowned. So, okay, maybe he had to wear makeup for the television cameras. And maybe it didn't wash off that well in between sportscasts. Except tonight. Or maybe…

Pansy forgot all about small discrepancies. Jesse was walking around the hot tub, inadvertently giving her a glimpse of his, er…anatomy. Her mouth went dry, and, strangely enough, her hands got clammy. Go figure.

Her fingers slithered on the binoculars, but she managed to keep watching while Jesse propped a foot on the edge of the tub and vigorously rubbed the muscles of his thigh. Pansy thought she saw something bobble. But maybe it was only her binocs. She was definitely losing her grip.

Jesse's pose was making her labor like a marathon runner in sight of the finish line, unable to draw a deep breath. Finally he put her out of her misery by stepping into the hot tub and slipping low in the water. With a small splash and a casual sidelong glance, he moved out of view.

She inhaled, exhaled, refocused the glasses because she thought she spotted Jesse's toes, and forgot to inhale until she realized Jesse's so-called toes were just a browning palm frond.

After another minute of breathing exercises, she dropped the binoculars, blinking like an owl, feeling as though the glasses had pressed permanent rings around her eye sockets. Oh, boy. Branded for a Peeping Tom—no less than she deserved. She licked her damp upper lip, watched the sunroom a bit longer—just in case—and finally let go of the blinds. The slats clattered shut.

Limply, she slid down in the wing chair, almost squashing the sleeping cat against the armrest. "Oh, hell, Tux," she said, scooping up the unresponsive pet. "What have I done?'' Wonderingly, she touched her warm cheeks, knowing that this time she'd gone too far to turn back. Seeing as how after tonight she and Jesse were practically *intimate*, there were no two ways about it.

She'd simply *have* to use the love potion.

3

The man next door

"I HATE THIS HOUSE."

Peter Angelini, shaved and washed and pressed, looked across the breakfast table at his unshaved brother. "Then why'd you buy it?" he asked mildly. Jesse was always grouchy and abnormally grungy in the morning; it came from staying out so late. Pete had outgrown that sort of behavior himself, but it would take mighty strong magic to halt Jesse's campaign of swinging singlehood.

"The realtor, that's why." Jesse gulped black coffee. "She's a luscious babe. S'got slicker moves than the Laker Girls."

Pete folded the morning *Dispatch* open to the editorial page. "That's certainly what I look for in a realtor."

"Hell, Pete, give me a break. I was in a rush. The station wanted me to start right away, so I needed a place to live. And Tami did move the closing along as easy as you please."

"I'm sure you were *pleased*—" Pete cocked an expressive eyebrow "—but now you're stuck with two bedrooms you don't need." Not even Jesse needed three at once.

"I'll turn them into a workout room and a trophy room." Jesse yawned. "Don't complain, little brother. At least you've got a place to stay while your condo's being painted."

Pete looked up from reading a co-worker's dour opinions about the ravages of Mother Nature and the limits of Belle Terre's snowplow budget. "There's a two-bedroom penthouse available in my building, you know."

"Tami said houses are the better buy."

"For a family man." Pete's brows arched again as he glanced over the edge of the newspaper. "Or was she planning to make you one?"

Tipped back in his chair, Jesse held up his hands defensively. "Not on my watch."

"Right." Pete snorted and rattled the paper. "One peal of wedding bells and there's smoke coming from your heels. The girl's lucky if she gets a wave goodbye."

"Don't see you signing on the dotted line, either, little brother."

"I believe you're familiar with my age, *big* brother. I*'ve* still got plenty of time."

Ignoring the familiar refrain, Jesse picked up the sports page and squinted. "Tell your publisher they're using too small a type on the box scores."

Pete laughed. "You sound like Dad, grumbling in his easy chair about the contents of the evening paper."

Jesse's eyes narrowed. "Hell I do. And there's no way I should have to use bifocals at the age of thirty-two."

Pete shrugged.

"Damn. Maybe it is time to think about settling down, then." Jesse stretched his arms overhead, pondering Tami, his curvy, peppy, enthusiastic realtor. He scratched his bare brown chest, remembering the look of promise in the receptionist's Scandinavian blue eyes when he walked into the TV station each day. Then he slapped his washboard abs, thinking of all the taut bodies at his gym and the cheerleaders in flippy little skirts at the games he covered, and finally lingering over the lovely redhead at the anchor desk who was waiting on tenterhooks for him to ask her out. Maybe tonight was her lucky night....

"Naw," Jesse concluded. "I'm having too much fun to

settle down. But you, Pete, you're another case. You spend way too much time in the newspaper office—you could use a sweet little wife to lure you home."

Suddenly Pete got busy clearing the table of their jam jars and toast crusts. Fact was, he'd been thinking along the same lines himself lately. Devoting all his time to a daily sports column was no longer as satisfying as it once had been, and lately his apartment was beginning to seem lonely and empty rather than quiet and minimalistic—hence the new paint and other renovations. Still, he didn't see any reason to admit that to his brother. Jesse had so many girlfriends he'd likely start tossing the spares to Pete, and Pete didn't want Jesse's castoffs. He'd run second place to his brother often enough that he'd learned to forge his own path instead.

Funny thing, though. A race to the altar was probably the only race his competitive "older" brother wouldn't mind losing.

"And that's another reason why I hate this house," Jesse said as he got up from the table. He pointed out the window, past the wide deck that encircled the sunroom addition. In the next yard, a senior citizen in a topcoat and open, flapping galoshes was shuffling around in the snow, going from bird feeder to bird feeder with a bag of seed. "The crackpot next door feeds birds all year round. They make so much damn noise in the mornings I have to sleep with a pillow over my head."

Pete wasn't listening; he was staring out the small bay window above the sink. He whistled softly. "C'mere, Jess." He waved his brother over. "Tell me—who's that?"

Jesse leaped across the kitchen and tackled Pete around the waist, knocking them both to the floor out of window range. "Hot damn," he crowed, picking himself off the linoleum and extending a hand to his brother. "I've still got it."

Pete slapped the hand in a low five instead of taking it.

"Yeah, if you'd hit like that for the Packers they'd never've cut you." He levered himself up, his fingers gripping the ledge of the sink, occupied with something other than the ignominious end of Jesse's football career. Pete peered past the windowsill. The fine young woman he'd spotted climbing down the steps next door was now standing beside the fellow with the bird seed, bobbing her head as she talked. She looked like a Christmas elf in a bright red, fitted jacket and furry green mittens and ear-muffs. Sunshine glinted off her bouncy auburn curls.

"Don't let her see you," warned Jesse, lurking nearby with his shoulders hunched up to his ears, ready to give his brother another shove at the first sign of possible exposure. "At least she doesn't have the binoculars out."

Pete's head snapped around. "Binoculars?"

"I think she watches me."

"Oh." Pete wished he'd been warned; suddenly he felt a touch uneasy. "Uh, why? What's she after?"

"You know the type." Jesse grunted. "She thinks she wants me, but what she really wants are wedding bells."

"Really." Pete's last, lingering hope sank like a stone in a wishing well. He eyed the cute girl-next-door with regret, admiring her smooth peach cheeks, bright smile and dancing eyes. She was short, maybe five-two, but compact rather than delicate. Hers were the ripe curves of a mature woman who was ready and willing and waiting restlessly for Mr. Right. Lucky guy.

Looking at her, it was easy for Pete to guess that she was the type who'd been an enthusiastic fan of the football team in high school, but not necessarily a cheerleader. She would've been secretary of her senior class and head of the prom decorating committee. She'd probably studied English Lit at a state university, gone home early from frat parties, if she attended them at all, and had her first love affair with a studious engineering major. Now, on the long side of her twenties, she loved her job, but do-

nated lots of time to her church and community, did nee-
dlepoint, cooked a mean pot roast, played hopscotch with
the neighborhood kids on warm spring days and fur-
tively pored over bridal magazines, dreaming of her own
overdue happily-ever-after. She dated nice guys, secretly
hankered for bad boys and Marlboro men, and believed
that love was forever. She would make some fortunate
man an excellent wife.

In fact, she was precisely the kind of woman who could
easily satisfy the growing hunger of Pete's empty heart.

It was a shame she'd already fallen prey to Jesse's
brand of playboy charm.

"So." Pete inclined his head, watching as the young
woman waved goodbye to the elderly gent and walked
slowly toward the street, her shoulders facing front but
her head gradually twisting farther and farther to the side
as she scoured Jesse's Victorian house with a pair of
round, pleading, puppy-dog eyes. "You've…dated?"

Jesse pushed Pete aside when he leaned closer to the
window to keep the neighbor in sight. "Careful. Sometimes I think she's gone, but she's still there, lurking, waiting for me to poke my nose out the door. Then she
pounces."

"How bad could that be?"

Jesse shrugged. "She's so cheerful it hurts."

"She asks you out?"

"Nope. Not the type. But she wants to. I can tell."

Pete swore inwardly. Jesse had all the luck.

"I made the mistake of dating her three times. Once
was enough to know we weren't compatible, but there
was something so darn *nice* about her…I couldn't figure
out how to break it off." Jesse grinned. "You'll be happy
to know that for once I was a gentleman."

Pete's expression brightened. "I'd calculate that had
more to do with her than you."

Jesse stuck his thumbs in the waistband of his gray

sweatpants and struck one of his handsome, young-jock-turned-sportscaster poses. "Oh, I don't know about that. The ladies say I'm pretty irresistible."

"Funny thing—they never say the same about me."

"That's 'cause you're the solid, marrying type." Jesse flicked his chin at the house next door. "So's she. If you're interested, I could maybe arrange an introduction."

Maybe, Pete thought. "What's her name?"

"Pansy Kingsmith. She lives in the attic apartment. But fair warning, little brother. She's the kind of girl a sap like you can't help falling in love with."

4

That evening at Pansy's place

THE HOT TUB!

The thought struck Pansy toward the end of the six o'clock WKSS newscast, startling her so much she neglected the rest of the scores Jesse was reading. Not that she cared whether the Bucks had won or lost, but she did like to feast her eyes on Jesse's wavy nut-brown hair and cleft chin, and marvel at how his perfect lips and come-hither baritone could make the phrases "one on one" and "full-court press" sound sinfully sexy.

Too excited to let Jesse finish his sports report, Pansy zapped off the television set and turned to her best friend and fellow NatureWords editor, Jane Kenton. "Jane. Jesse Angelini has a hot tub! I don't know why I didn't think of it sooner."

Dishwater-blond Jane, as plain as her name, looked up from scouring pea pods out of the bottom of a Chinese take-out container. She crinkled her eyes behind a pair of serious tortoiseshell-frame glasses. "You wouldn't dare."

Together, they looked at the vial of Angel Water sitting in the exact center of the round, pickled-pine dining table. The setting sun had bathed the dormered dining area with a tawny golden light.

The apricot liquid of the love potion seemed to beckon Pansy with an eerie, incandescent glow. Her palms itched to hold it. She rose from her chair by the TV and went to pick up the vial, then immediately got nervous and set it down with the utmost care. Vaguely aware of Jane's level gaze tracking her, Pansy paced the length of the apartment, wringing her hands. Jesse had a hot tub. He used it often, even in winter, as last night had proved. She could sneak next door and empty the vial into the tub. If she missed her chance to-night, there was sure to be another opportunity—and another full moon.

On the other hand, if she didn't go through with it tonight, she might come back to her senses and then she'd *never* dare to try something as outlandish as se-duction-by-love-potion.

The plan that was forming in her mind was so sim-ple it was scary. If the love potion worked, Jesse wouldn't know what hit him. And if it didn't, no one but herself and Jane—whom Pansy trusted implic-itly—would be the wiser.

Of course, it wasn't going to work. Pansy wasn't fooling herself on that point. But after going over it in her mind that morning at work, and finally confessing all to Jane over their brown-bag lunch, she'd come to the conclusion that limiting herself to the straight and narrow was pretty darn boring. Look what a thrill Jesse's inadvertent peep show had given her. Actually dumping a so-called love potion into his hot tub would *really* spice things up!

Whether or not it actually had an effect.

But, oh, boy, what if it did?

She had to be extremely careful with thoughts like that. Allowing a little whimsy into her life might be okay. Letting it balloon to the point where fantasy was more involving than reality wasn't.

Pansy stopped and stared out the dormer window with the best view of Jesse's house, reminding herself to keep her boots planted firmly in the snow. Even while she was scaling the fence into his backyard.

"I'm going to do it," she told Jane with a trembly, growing conviction. "I'm going to sneak over to Jesse's hot tub and pour the Angel Water into it and see what happens!"

"You're kidding." Jane shook her head, accustomed to playing anchor to the crazy ideas that occasionally whipped up out of nowhere and sent Pansy's resolution to be levelheaded soaring off into the stratosphere. She scooped up another chunk of sesame chicken and, chewing, said heavily, "Nuh-uh, you'll never go through with it."

Pansy put her hands on her hips. "And why not?"

Jane shrugged. "Neither of us is the spontaneous type."

"I've deliberately tried not to be," Pansy conceded. "Maybe too hard."

Jane just kept dipping in and out of the carton, her skinny legs slung over the arm of a worn floral-tapestry chair that had once been a Le Junque window display special. She swallowed and tapped the chopsticks into alignment on her kneecap, pursing her lips as she considered the possibilities. "Nope, I don't see it. Even if you could go through with such a far-fetched stunt, there's still everything that might go wrong. How can you tell when Jesse will use the hot tub? What if he stays late to do the ten o'clock news, like last night? Or what if he comes home early and catches you—"

Pansy turned. "I didn't know you watched Jesse's show."

Jane shut her mouth and shrugged wordlessly, gone pink around the edges.

"And he did not do the sports last night. I told you, he was in the hot tub. Remember?" Pansy grew warm just thinking of it. "Besides, Jane, for once I don't want to think about what can go wrong. Now is not the time to be sensible."

Not even Jane could bring herself to disagree. She'd already promised to support Pansy's decision even if her own practicality about these things kept her from showing too much enthusiasm. And as she was secretly nurturing her own small crush on Jesse, she understood Pansy's motive. Sometimes a woman was so crazy in love she'd grasp at that one chance in a million.

"Well, then...I wish you luck." Jane's chopsticks scraped the bottom of the carton. She looked inside, licked the last grain of rice off the tip of her finger and carefully piled the take-out cartons in a neat pyramid atop the cedar chest coffee table. She got up, displacing enough air to topple the cartons. "Sorry," she said, picking them up again. "Whaddya know? They forgot the fortune cookies again—story of my life." She slipped into her coat and hiked a hefty canvas army backpack onto her shoulders, hunching under the weight of the book she was editing: *The Encyclopedia of Earthworms*. Mr. Barney would be rapturous when he got his hands on it.

"Jane—stay," Pansy blurted. Her eyebrows squinched together in apprehension. "I can't do this alone!"

"Nuh-uh," Jane said, slowly straightening, "you're not roping me into this. You know me—I'd probably fall into the hot tub or something and ruin the whole thing." She rolled her eyes. "Weaken the spell."

Pansy cast her friend a pleading look. Unrelenting, Jane smoothed her hair behind her ears, the corners of her lips tucked into a sorry-no-thanks smile. Pansy was about to start pleading in earnest when a light went on in Jesse's house.

"He's home!" She leapt toward the dormer window,

unceremoniously nudging Tux out of his favorite spot on the cabbage-rose-patterned wing chair. Kneeling on the seat and peeping over the backrest as she had the night before, she followed Jesse's movements through his downstairs rooms. He stopped to turn on a light in the kitchen. "Hmm, that was quick," Pansy murmured.

Tapping on the face of her wristwatch, Jane counted back the minutes to his sportscast. "Nearly impossible, I'd say. How'd he get home so fast?"

Tux mewed and started kneading the back of Pansy's calves. Absentmindedly she picked the cat up and slid down to the seat, her thoughts churning. Jesse did have a racy red sports car, and he did drive very fast. Unfortunately, his garage and driveway were on the other side of his house where she couldn't see them.

"Are you sure that's Jesse Angelini?" Jane asked, craning her neck to see through the window. She took off her glasses and squinted.

"Of course I'm sure. He's lived next door to me for seven months and eight days, so I think I'd know by now...." Even so, Pansy dumped Tux off her lap and twisted around the arm of the chair, dropping her chin to peer inside the kitchen window. Jesse stood near the sink, abnormally absorbed with the newspaper, the light shining directly upon his thick brown hair. True, the hair didn't seem as styled and blow-dried as it had on TV, but the face was definitely Jesse's. Definitely. Just slightly less tan.

But so handsome. Pansy sighed, pressing her cheek against the curve of the wing chair.

Obviously recognizing the signs of an oncoming reverie about Jesse's many attributes, Jane pushed her glasses back up her nose and said, "Okay, so I guess this is where I say goodbye."

Pansy barely murmured in response, too focused on Jesse to stop Jane's departure. Her friend appeared outside, stepping down the stairway with one hand on the icy railing and the other easing the drag on the shoulder strap of her backpack. Jane's appearance caught Jesse's attention through his kitchen window. When she turned, he nodded in greeting, smiling in the vaguely friendly way you do to a stranger. That was a little odd. But then, Pansy decided, he'd only been introduced to Jane once, on the fly. And Jane was, in her own words, not especially memorable. She was the type of person who blended in.

Suddenly Jesse looked up, straight at Pansy's window. With a cry of surprise she ducked out of sight, then dared a second peek and was almost caught again. She slumped dramatically, hands pressed to her blushing cheeks. "Close call, Tux. He almost caught me that time."

The regal cat flicked his ears, turned and stalked across the apartment with his tail straight up and the tip twitching spasmodically. He leapt onto the high bed, expressly ignoring Pansy's antics.

She scrambled to her feet and dropped the blinds, then couldn't resist lifting one corner for another peek. Jesse was no longer in sight, but her heartbeat thundered as if he was right beside her. She *could* be spontaneous and daring, no matter what Jane—and Pansy's own cautious nature—said.

She tried to bolster her decision. Even though Jane had chickened out on her, the rest of the situation remained ideal. For one, Jesse was home early. For another, the hot tub was already warmed up from last night, making it entirely possible that he'd decide to use it again. Her only problem would be sneaking into the sunroom without his seeing her. And sneaking out again, unless she intended to take in another strip show from an even more advantageous position than the night before.

To stop the spreading of the throbbing warmth that always accompanied thoughts of Jesse in the altogether, Pansy stared at the vial of love potion and thought serious thoughts about getting caught and going to jail. Jane would have to bail her out. Word would spread. Her embarrassment would be extreme, her reputation undone. But at least she'd have taken a chance instead of just moping by the window while Jesse worked his way through Wisconsin's entire populace of eligible women.

Pansy became resolute. Yes, she *could* do it! In only a few hours the moon would be high and full and all aglow, casting its indefinable allure over the mysteries of the human psyche.

The night would be ripe for romance.

5

Rendezvous with destiny, via hot tub

BECAUSE PANSY WAS so short, the wrought-iron fence around Jesse's yard came up to her ribs. It wasn't difficult to climb, only awkward, what with a minibackpack slewing between her shoulder blades and her binoculars clanking against the fence. The bill of her cap slid down over her eyes as she mounted the snowbank and slung one leg over the fence to straddle it like a bronc rider. The spade-shaped spires poked at her in very rude ways, so she hurriedly swung her second leg over and dropped down on the other side, landing in a squat behind the snow-covered clump of a hydrangea bush.

She'd already reconnoitered the situation from her balcony. With Mr. Barney's binoculars, she'd watched while Jesse zapped a frozen dinner in the microwave, ate it in the kitchen with only the newspaper for company and then spent almost an hour in an easy chair with his back to her, flipping channels on the TV until he settled on ESPN. She'd been about ready to give up the ghost when finally he'd risen and gone out to the sunroom to ready the hot tub. When he went back inside, she'd stashed the love potion and the velvet pouch in her backpack and raced down the stairs and across the yard with her heart in her mouth. She recognized a window of opportunity when she spied one.

Pansy hesitated behind the hydrangea, watching the light that had gone on upstairs. Jesse must be changing. *Or stripping down to nothing but his perfect smile,* she thought with a spiraling heat that made her squirm in her boots. Either way, this was her best chance to do the deed.

Without stopping to reflect on the more ridiculous aspects of her scheme, she darted across the snowy yard and climbed the stairs to the wooden deck off the sunroom. Stealthily, she skirted the lattice panels twined with dormant ivy and tried the glass door. It opened with a tug, scraping an arc through the fresh snow. Unlocked doors were still common in Belle Terre; word about marauding love-potion bandits hadn't yet hit the streets.

Pansy glanced up at the lit window to double-check Jesse's whereabouts before she stepped inside the tiled sunroom. Hooking the backpack off her shoulders, she brushed past the potted palms and deck chairs and went straight to the hot tub, which was bubbling like a witch's cauldron.

Bubble, bubble, toil and trouble, she thought, peeling off her black leather gloves and unzipping the backpack to retrieve the precious frosted-glass vial. Stifling a nervous giggle, she tugged on the cork stopper. It clung stubbornly in the narrow bottleneck. Feeling frantic, she yanked.

The cork popped out and flew into the hot tub, where it sank, then bobbed back to the surface, then disappeared again in the roiling water. After briefly trying to follow its tumultuous ride through the bubbles, Pansy decided that the prudent course was to abandon the cork rather than try to fish it out. Judging by Jesse's past hot tub habits, should he notice the stopper as it bobbed past, he'd probably assume it had come from one of his own bottles of wine or champagne.

A radio was switched on inside the house, and dialed to a classic rock station instead of Jesse's usual sports talk show. Whatever, it meant that he was likely to reappear at any moment. She had to be quick!

Pansy tipped the vial over the hot tub. In a pale, orangey gold stream, the Angel Water merged with the hot, bubbling froth, instantly dissipating so that Jesse would never guess that magic was being worked upon him while he soaked.

Mission accomplished. Pansy sobered now that it was done. The outcome was irrevocable; she could only pray that it was also favorable.

Remembering the agate, she put down the bottle and reached into the minibackpack for the black velvet pouch. A pair of loafers lay beside one of the deck chairs—as if fate had put them there. It was almost enough to make one believe....

Operating on instinct, Pansy kissed the agate. She knelt and with trembling fingers poked it deep into the toe of one of the creased, scuffed shoes. A tiny question nagged at her; she tried to push it out of her mind. Jesse was a sharp dresser, with quite an array of expensive, polished shoes to his name, yet she'd seen him out here just now with her own two eyes. With her own binoculars, even. So these *must* be his shoes, even if he didn't usually go in for the beat-up, casual look except when he crawled out of bed in the morning. Then he wasn't wearing shoes at all, just a pair of gray sweatpants that clung to his slim hips in a very interesting way.

Pansy straightened, frowning at the shoe in her hand.

"Well, hi, there."

Startled, she dropped the shoe with a thud. Jesse stood in the doorway that led to the dining room, watching her, and even though he'd sounded friendlier than he had for some time, he also looked taken aback, studying her with his brow furrowed as though he was trying to decide if she was a burglar or just another groupie. "Did I miss your knock?" he asked, reaching inside to flick on the sunroom lights.

In the instant that he was turned toward the wall switch, Pansy snatched up her backpack and dropped the

velvet drawstring bag inside it. She didn't have time to retrieve the vial because already Jesse was bounding down
the steps toward her, holding out his hand as if this was
the first time they'd met.

"Pansy Kingsmith?" he said, smiling a smile that
nearly made her knees buckle. Suddenly everything was
happening in slow motion, so slow she had time to notice
that one of Jesse's front teeth was slightly crooked—how
had she missed such a winsome imperfection?—and that
his navy blue robe was untied over a pair of baggy ma-
dras trunks—which saved her from complete physical
distress—and that he seemed so much *nicer* than she remembered.

If she'd had some small doubts about the wisdom of
her scheme—after all, there was the distinct possibility
that Jesse's heart wasn't in accord with hers—they vanished in the touch of his hand on hers and the lazy sweep
of his brown lashes as he looked her up and down. Ap-
preciatively, which was a nice change from his recent
wariness.

"Of course it's me," she said, her voice floating out of
her open mouth like the curls of steam off the hot tub. She
faltered. Was the lengthy string of women that Jesse
maintained so extensive that he had to search his mind for
her name? That could get annoying pretty fast. "I live
next door," she added for clarification, half-sarcastic as
the moment snapped back into real time. Leagues of gorgeous rivals had a way of doing that to a girl.

"I know."

"Well, I remember you, too," she said, wholly sarcastic,
just to show him that maybe she wasn't a total feeb. She
put her hand on her forehead and squinted as if straining
her brain. "I even recall your name."

"Oh. Well." Jesse smiled, his eyes so piercingly blue
they outshone the unnatural aquamarine glow of the hot
tub. "I guess my brother explained about—"

"I don't have time to chat." Pansy waved off whatever excuse he was concocting to explain his recent neglectful behavior. Blaming his brother, was he? Well, after tonight, if the love potion worked, what had gone before would no longer matter.

She backed toward the glass door, slipping her arms through the straps of the shiny black vinyl backpack. Thank heaven Jesse had chosen not to skinny-dip. Even close up and half-clothed, his body was an awesome sight—aesthetic, athletic, with all that lickable skin stretched taut over his long, muscled frame. She wanted to zap back into slow motion and kiss him all over for hours on end, but she was having a hard time overlooking the awfulness of the hot tub looming behind him. It was a steaming, churning symbol of her gullible naiveté. Evidence of her ultimate foolishness.

Jesse made a questioning gesture. "But why—"

Pansy remembered she was an intruder. "I thought I saw a magpie in your tree, so I had to check it out because, well, my friend lost her pet magpie and we're worried it's going to freeze, being outside in the winter." She indicated the binoculars dangling around her neck, pleased with her quick thinking until she realized she hadn't explained why she was *inside.* "And then, I, er…" Her brain froze. She couldn't come up with even a lame excuse, so she smiled hugely and hoped he wouldn't ask. "Please excuse me for intruding. I'll let myself out the gate. You go on back to your—" her eyes darted over his bare chest, the smattering of swirl-patterned hair there "—er, your hot tub." She turned rosy as a red-breasted nuthatch and bolted off the deck. Thankfully Jesse didn't follow as she sped toward the front gate, her face hot and her previously dominant practical half berating her suddenly out-of-control insensible half.

You are certifiably nuts. Completely off your rocker. Crazy-

fool in love with a man who looks at you as if you'd never even met before.

And there was nothing for her to do about it but sit back and wait to see what would happen next.

CLIMBING INTO THE WATER to ease the sore muscles he'd earned in a straight week of lunch hour squash games with his brother, Peter Angelini spied the frosted-glass bottle set on the ledge. He knew at once that Pansy Kingsmith had left it. The sixty-four-thousand-dollar question was *why?* Although she'd claimed to be bird-watching or some such, he hadn't believed her for an instant. Beneath the brim of a green-and-white Packers' Super Bowl cap, her pretty face had been too open and guileless—and definitely too flushed—to defend the lie.

Pete had been on the verge of asking if she'd like to join him in the hot tub when she'd hightailed it back to safety, her breasts full and round beneath a black wool sweater, the dinky backpack bouncing above a pert, curvy derriere encased in tight black jeans. She'd looked like a burstingly healthy farmer's daughter's version of *La Femme Nikita*, and he'd regretted his moment of hesitation before the invitation. Certainly Jesse would've dived in headfirst, and been so smooth about it he'd have had Pansy naked and neck deep in hot water before she could refuse.

But Pete wasn't Jesse, even though they looked so much alike, and he'd grown wise enough to see that at times discretion—the cautious man's word for hesitation—was called for. Unfortunately, this probably hadn't been one of those times, because now he was alone. And so was Pansy.

Pretty Pansy, with her cinnamon curls and pink cheeks and ripe curves. Her eyes, big and brown and beseeching.

He picked up the empty bottle, shook it and peered inside, sniffing. He caught a whiff of a faint, exotic perfume. Bath oil, he thought, wondering if the Pansy-next-door had intended to surprise Jesse in the hot tub until *he'd* come out and she'd realized he wasn't Jesse at all.

It wasn't that Pete wanted to *be* Jesse. At least not since he'd turned twenty-five or so and had finally grown into his hormones.

As far as women were concerned, Jesse was a heart-throb, a Romeo; Pete was a good guy, a friendly shoulder to lean on. Jesse had been a sports star throughout high school, college and, for several glamorous years, the pros; Pete had been an adequate second-stringer until he'd realized he preferred reporting on the games than playing in them. Jesse was smooth; Pete was sincere. Jesse believed in living fast, rolling with the punches, playing by ear; Pete had come to believe that a man's word was his honor, and that time went too fast not to slow down and appreciate the finer things.

Jesse's finer things were hot dates and expensive cars; Pete's were tied up with one warm sweetheart of a woman who didn't mind that a sports columnist could only afford a four-year-old sedan.

Jesse was pleased with the way his life had turned out. So was Pete.

Even so…Pete had to acknowledge that although he wouldn't trade identities with his brother, Jesse really did have all the luck. And all the girls.

Even the ones he didn't want.

6

The witching hour

PANSY HAD DOZED OFF while she waited for Jesse. After watching from the window until he'd disappeared behind the lattice that screened the better part of the hot tub, she'd prepared for their potential rendezvous—showering, powdering, primping.

It always pays to be prepared, she soothed herself, trying not to dwell on what exactly she was preparing *for* as she slipped a floaty yellow nightie over her head. Tux sat on the bed, watching her with his knowing green eyes. She shooed him away.

Okay, while it was true that she wasn't accustomed to acting like a sexually aggressive woman, there was a chance, a million-in-one chance, that the love potion would work. And if it did, all other bets would be off. In Jesse's eyes, she'd be transformed....

When the knocking finally sounded at her door hours later, she was asleep, curled on her side with Tux nestled in the crook of her knees. The negligee was a crinkled mess, twisted around her hips and crushed between her thighs. She leaped out of bed and smoothed it down, trying, with limited success, to go from muzzy and befuddled to sultry and welcoming. Tux lay on his side and stretched, leaving black cat hairs all over the comforter.

"C-come in," Pansy warbled around the lump in her throat, hoping the light from the candles she'd set around the room was weak enough to disguise the worst of her and the cat's dishabille. Luckily, half the candles had already burned down to the nub.

The door swung open.

Jesse stood there like an apparition of the cold, black night, the full moon hovering over his shoulder, hung low above the mansard roof next door. He was wearing the loafers with the agate in the toe, no socks, khaki pants wet with snow and a bomber jacket unzipped over a T-shirt, his wavy brown hair tumbled across his forehead. He looked at Pansy, then down at the empty love potion vial in his hand, appearing stunned to find himself shivering on her doorstep. And clearly uncertain about what to do next.

He raked a hand through his hair. "I know it's late."

Propelled by an impulse she could no longer squelch, Pansy flew into his arms. "I've been waiting for you!"

His arms went around her waist even though he continued to regard her quizzically. "For me? You've been waiting for *me*?"

"I knew you'd come, darling." She licked her lips and threw back her head in the manner of the cover models on her favorite romance novels. Unfortunately, her matted curls clung to her moist neck like the frizz of a poodle instead of falling down her back in a silken swath of fiery waves.

"Uh, I brought your bottle—"

"You don't have to explain," she said, wrapping her arms around his neck to urge him closer to her eager lips. "I know why you're here." Either she was hyperventilating or her bosom was actually heaving—she did feel rather overwrought. And though she'd never been known to behave rashly, she couldn't prevent herself from adding fervently, "Kiss me, my darling!"

"Hold on, there, Pansy," Jesse said, uncharacteristically hesitant. "You've got me all wrong."

"I know what I'm doing," she insisted. *Or what the love*

potion was doing, she silently amended. Practically the same thing.

"You've got me there, because I can promise I haven't a clue."

Pansy's exalted expression was growing strained. Jesse wasn't acting very Jesse-like, but then who knew what physiological changes had been induced by the love potion? Come to think of it, under other circumstances she would have appreciated that for once he was considering the consequences instead of obeying the demands of rampaging testosterone.

But under *these* circumstances, she wanted him to shut up and kiss her like a properly besotted victim of aphrodisia.

Acting quickly before she could succumb to her own insecurities, Pansy grabbed the bottle from Jesse and tossed it aside. She took both of his hands in hers and led him to the studio apartment's bedroom alcove. A few of the candles still shone from the nightstands, making her tall, whitewashed pine four-poster bed with its plump Pottery Barn duvet look very cozy and inviting.

Jesse stared, a little slow on the uptake considering that bedroom seductions were his milieu more than hers.

Pansy hesitated. *Well, sometimes a gal's gotta do what a gal's gotta do....*

She crawled to the center of the bed, the long negligee dragging beneath her knees. Gathering the filmy fabric in her lap, she sat back on her heels and smiled a shy invitation at Jesse. Hopefully he was getting the idea and would take it from here.

"You don't know..." Jesse's blue eyes seemed stuck on the place where the lace-edged strap had fallen off her shoulder. He licked his lips and shrugged out of his jacket. "You don't know who I am."

Of course Pansy knew. She'd been observing him for months now. But she kept smiling, determined to baby him along if that was what it took. He was bound to be somewhat discombobulated by his sudden, overwhelming attraction to her. "I know that I want you," she said.

He moaned under his breath. "I want you, too."

That was the best news she'd heard all night. She patted the bed, turning Tux back with a glare when the cat tensed to spring into Jesse's intended place. "Please join me," she purred, watching out of the corner of her eye as Tux turned away in whisker-twitching disgust.

Despite his better instincts, Pete was strongly tempted to accept. "I'm not sure that I can resist," he said, mainly to himself. Resisting was the gentlemanly thing to do, but... He thrust his hands into his pockets and found in one of them the unusual rock he'd fished from his shoe. He clutched it as though it was a talisman. "There seems to be a powerful force overtaking all my objections."

Pansy's eyes widened. "Then it's working."

Pete leaned down to put his palms flat against the periwinkle duvet, bringing his face in line with hers. "Something's working. Something I've never felt before."

"Do you feel an overwhelming desire for me?" she asked disingenuously, blinking her big brown eyes at him.

"Absolutely." Guilt caught in his throat. "But there's something I have to tell you."

Pansy didn't seem to want to hear it. She held his face in her hands and pressed her lips to his, making a tiny, welcoming sound in her throat. And suddenly he was sinking down onto the bed, with her all warm and round and silky beneath him. "Later," she panted, her eyes and lips glistening invitingly. "We'll talk later."

That sounded like a plan to Pete. A scoundrel's plan, but good Lord, how could he object when she was serving herself up to him like a piece of fluffy lemon meringue pie? Couldn't he just this once ignore his conscience and do the wrong thing? Do it even though he knew he shouldn't because this time it felt too damn good to stop?

Then Pansy was kissing him again and he wasn't stopping her. Instead he was kissing her back, and kissing her front, and kissing her cheeks and the hollow in her throat and the freckled strawberries-and-cream slope of her breasts, pressed full and round in the low neckline of her sexy negligee. He cupped his hands over her breasts, marveling at her softness, her giving, cushioning, endless softness. Aching little whimpers sounded in her throat when he stroked her nipples through the sheer fabric and put his mouth there and then his tongue, sweeping it deep into her cleavage and around the edge of the neckline until the straps had worked their way down her arms. Then her breasts were revealed, bountiful treasures, and her nipples, rubbing across his lips, teasing him mercilessly until he opened wide and sucked one of them inside his hot mouth, making her pedal her feet against the bed and shiver with pleasure.

They broke apart, both of them agape. "It's working," Pansy said with wonder. "It's really working!"

Which made no sense to Pete. But he couldn't think beyond the raging physical instinct of all that he wanted to do to her, *was* doing to her, his mouth locked on hers, his hands roaming wildly. Without a speck of hesitation, he pushed her negligee up around her waist and she didn't protest. On the contrary, she seemed to like it, so he obligingly lifted the daffodil-colored gown off over her head. She lay back, quivering as he stroked a path up her sleek, powdered thighs to find the damp heat flowering beneath the thin silk of her matching yellow panties. The sight of those panties nearly undid him. Pansy was so girlish and sweet and trusting, and at the same time so womanly and ripe and ready. He was tormented, but not enough to put a stop to what she'd begun.

Pansy was astonished at herself—and at how quickly

she squirmed out of her underpants. This was not like her, not at all, but her body was aflame with a need that flickered between her thighs and burned all the way up to the melting cravings of her heart. Thanks to the Angel Water, Jesse was here at last to quench the flames. She could hardly believe it was true!

But it had to be, because she was helping him slide out of his clothes, both of them fumbling with haste until at last his broad male body was pressed heavily against her, his hard, hot flesh coaxing her to yield, though she didn't have to be asked. She was shockingly eager.

His kisses overwhelmed her. He teased her with his dancing fingertips and his talented mouth until she was limp with lust and he had to slide his palms around her bottom and lift her up to meet the plunge of his hips. Their bodies merged, the gliding thrust of their union welcomed by a mutual, bone-deep, shuddering sigh of relief.

Pansy's eyes welled. Being with Jesse was better than she'd imagined. It was like coming home after a lifetime of journeying alone.

She licked his lips, she pressed her tongue against his, she spoke his name into his open mouth and then sealed it with her own when he tried to speak. He rocked against her, his hands squeezing her bottom, his forehead rubbing against the bridge of her nose as he put his head down and moved deeply inside her. Their clinging, wet, messy kisses ebbed and flowed in concert with each tug of their mysteriously strong connection.

Oh—the Angel Water! Pansy remembered, half-wild with gratitude.

The pressure and passion built exquisitely. She rolled her head back and surrendered to it, writhing, first grabbing handfuls of the duvet, then clutching at Jesse with her fingers and her thighs and her entire pleading body. She stared into his riveting blue eyes until everything went blurry as finally the hot ecstasy of her fantasy-come-true escalated beyond control and burst into a climax that shook her body from tingling scalp to trembling toes.

"Jesse," she said prayerfully, wanting only to string his name into a litany of desire. He made a harsh sound in his throat and shuddered violently with his own release. She arched against him, their bodies sliding, squirming, slickened by sweat. She licked her tongue over his shoulder. "Oh, Jesse…"

"No." He pressed his face against her breasts, his lips hot on her damp skin. She caught her breath, stricken, but then he was saying, "I think maybe I love you," his voice hoarse in her ear as he turned her over on her side and dropped into place behind her. His arms twined around her waist and she melted against him, soft and warm with satisfaction. "And I don't know how or why it could happen so fast."

She could have done without that last part, even though she did know how. *Particularly* because she knew how. The uncomfortable knowledge interfered with what should have been a moment of complete bliss.

"It must have been something in the water," she said, trying to keep the mood light and upbeat. Men were supposed to prefer that…afterward. She couldn't, for instance, grab Jesse tight and tell him that she wanted to be his wife.

"The water?"

She savored the wonderfully unique feel of his naked body pressed against hers, hard and large and comforting. If only she didn't have to think about what had lured him into her bed. If only she alone had been enough to put him there!

"The hot tub," she answered. "You started getting this overwhelming desire for me after you got into the hot tub, right, Jesse?"

He tightened. "Pansy, there's something I have to tell you."

Pansy's skin twitched. Something was nagging at her consciousness, sending her gaze to the dormer window across the room. The winter sky glittered with stars; the moon was luminous and full as a silver dollar. Adderley Avenue was so quiet it gradually dawned on Pansy that she could hear soft music, splashing water and a mixture of provocative male and female laughter coming from the house next door. From the sunroom. From Jesse Angelini's hot tub!

Which was impossible! She bolted upright. He was right here beside her in bed.

Jesse—her Jesse—pulled on his pants and slid to the edge of the mattress, fumbling with his zipper. She was reassured when she saw the small red birthmark below his shoulder blade. But then he said, "Please let me explain."

Pansy wrapped herself in the thick duvet; suddenly she was shivering with alarm. Despite the possibility of an answer she didn't want to hear, she croaked, "Who's in the hot tub?"

"I think it's Jesse—"

"*Jesse!*"

"And the anchorwoman from his station. Her name is Claudia. Claudia something…"

"Jesse," Pansy repeated through clenched teeth. "Jesse." She didn't want to believe any of the impossible possibilities that were suddenly spilling through her mind.

"But you're Jesse." Her lips trembled. "Aren't you…?"

The man who looked exactly like Jesse, the man the love potion had cast a spell over—*sweet heaven, the man she'd just made love with!*—stood and gestured helplessly. "I thought my brother had told you. I thought you knew…."

Pansy paled. "You and Jesse. You and Jesse are—you're—" A likely truth hit her, making her cringe with dread. "No-o-o," she moaned. "You and Jesse can't be twins!"

7

The aftermath

HOW COULD I HAVE KNOWN? Pansy railed impotently as she stalked around the apartment. She threw a pillow across the room, sending poor Tux scrambling under the bed for cover. Jesse had mentioned a brother, but he'd never said a word about them being twins. Why, he'd even called Peter Angelini his *little* brother. She was certain of it!

She'd never have risked putting the love potion into the hot tub if she'd had an inkling that just anyone would be hopping into it like they belonged there. Including Claudia Whomever—the recipient of all the proper *Jesse* Angelini Angel Water benefits that should have been Pansy's.

Strangely enough, Peter had said—just before she tossed him out—that he'd barely stuck his legs into the water when finding the vial had stopped him. Then Jesse and Claudia had arrived unexpectedly and he'd left the hot tub to them. Pansy didn't know how the love potion would work in such a tangled situation. Surely it took more than Peter's half-a-dip to produce results. Which meant that maybe he hadn't been operating under the influence of an aphrodisiac at all when he'd come over to return the empty bottle. Which meant...

Mortified, Pansy collapsed on the bed face first. Talk

about your bottle-return deposits. She'd given a complete stranger quite the bonus for returning this one!

Damn. No wonder he'd seemed reluctant…at first. Why had she acted so rashly? Why hadn't she listened to her head when in her experience impulsiveness always led to disaster? Why had she thrown herself at a veritable stranger and made love like a woman possessed?

Pansy couldn't blame her own imprudent actions on the love potion, only on wishful thinking and too many nights alone. But then she hadn't done it entirely on her own. Peter Angelini had participated enthusiastically, whether or not he'd intended to when he came to her door.

Come to think of it, he could have been entertaining certain hopes of his own, knocking on her door at such a late hour. It could be that he was genuinely attracted to her. Stranger things had happened.

She lifted her head, eyes brightening, then abruptly decided no. There was still the agate. She'd almost forgotten about the agate.

It must have been the lowly little agate she'd placed in the toe of Jesse's twin's loafers that had led the wrong man to her bed.

And Peter *was* the wrong man; there should be no doubt about that.

With a moan, Pansy rolled over and stared up at the angled ceiling. How perfectly terrible, and how perfectly predictable that her one attempt at sorcery had been a complete disaster. She might as well have let her nutty mother conjure up a potion on her kitchen stove for all the good the Angel Water had done her.

Pansy's first mistake had been allowing the encounter with Mademoiselle Grimaldi to get her hopes up. The second had been letting her little crush on Jesse blow up to absurd proportions. But now that she had

remembered who she was—and who she was not—
what could she do to clean up the mess?

Nothing.

She'd simply have to accept that the love potion
hadn't worked, at least not on the right people. The
thing with the agate was a…coincidence. There was no
proof that it had exerted any influence.

Except for that which her own body offered. Pansy
closed her eyes and ran her hand along her abdomen,
remembering the deep pleasure Peter's touch had
given her. How she'd felt completed by their joining.

But she'd been fooled. And her body had been
fooled. Her only consolation was that maybe in a
month, or a year, or five, she would forget that any of
this had happened.

Her wandering fingertips grazed one of her sensitive
breasts. She bit her lip. Maybe in ten years she'd forget.…

For now, though, there was no avoiding the fact that
making love with Peter Angelini had been fabulous.
Even if she'd thought he was Jesse. Which made her
wonder…would it be better with Jesse? Her skin was
still prickling with delicious aftershocks, so she
doubted that such a thing was possible. That left only
one option.

Unless twins were interchangeable, she and Jesse
had never been meant to be together. Her crush on him
had been woefully misguided.

What, then, of Peter? Was her mistake with the agate
not really a mistake? Had their meeting been predes-
tined by Mademoiselle Grimaldi?

Pansy rolled over onto her stomach again and
slammed her fists against the bed. She was thinking
nonsense. She was. And she had to stop it.

Yet, when she closed her eyes, a handsome, familiar
face popped into her mind, and this time she didn't

know if it belonged to Peter or Jesse any more than she was able to stop the cravings of her body or the drift of her increasingly uncontrolled thoughts. Thoughts that kept turning involuntarily to what Peter had said, despite the fact that he'd said it in the heat of the moment: "I think maybe I love you."

Could the power of one measly little agate put those words in his mouth? And why did a good part of her yearn to return the sentiment even though he wasn't at all—or at least not entirely—the man she'd intended to enchant?

JESSE AND PETER ANGELINI sat at the dining table, both of them silent and confused, and also, admittedly, strangely pleased, though still hiding their dazed faces behind sheets of the morning newspaper. Finally Jesse tired of staring at smudged newsprint. He put the paper down, picked up a toasted bagel and smeared it with peanut butter. Chewing, he gazed dopily in the direction of the hot tub.

Peter continued staring just as dopily at the newspaper. He was seeing Pansy, a nakedly pink and writhing Pansy, an erotic, X-rated Pansy, a Pansy with glazed eyes and tousled hair and a mouth as sweet as a honeycomb and a body as hot as a sauna. But then he was seeing the other Pansy, the one who'd been shocked and disbelieving and deeply mortified that she'd made love to an imposter. The one who'd told him to get out and leave her alone and never, never come near her again.

Behind the newspaper, Pete leaned his forehead against the heel of his palm. He'd deserved that. Although he'd tried to excuse himself by claiming that he thought she knew he wasn't Jesse, deep down he'd known all along that he was taking advantage of the situation. Pleading a sudden attack of overwhelming lust wasn't good enough.

It was mighty odd, though, how she'd gabbled on about the hot tub. "Something in the water," she'd said, and, "It's working." Apparently she was a lot kookier than appearances had led him to believe. She'd seemed to be expecting Jesse to appear at her apartment last night, although why, Pete couldn't imagine. Jesse had been pretty obvious about avoiding her.

And now Pete knew why, firsthand. His older twin—by twenty-three minutes—had always been a charmer, but a rogue when it came to women. He liked to say that he loved women, *many* women, and that was the way he intended to continue.

Whereas Pansy was the type of woman a man couldn't help falling in love with and committing to. Reason enough to send Jesse running in the other direction. And Pete directly to her bed.

Of course, he didn't really know her...in the non-biblical sense. But he'd like to. It would justify the fact that somehow, someway, against all common sense, he'd fallen in love with her.

All he had to do was come up with a way to approach her. If he waited a day or two or ten until she'd calmed down, he could possibly even persuade her to forgive his lapse in good judgment. And maybe then she'd consent to speak to him again.

He was hoping that the first thing she'd tell him was that she was over Jesse.

Jesse. Handsome, perfect Jesse.

Pete looked at his twin. There seemed to be only one way for things to come out right. Only one way that he'd know for sure who Pansy wanted.

"Jesse, are you doing anything for Valentine's Day?" he asked. "Because I may need a small favor from you...."

8

High noon on Nitschke Street

"HELLO? Mademoiselle Grimaldi?" Pansy knocked on the door of the love potion shop. "Please let me in."

Warily, she wrapped her fingers around the brass latch. It felt solid enough, so she tugged and jiggled it, pounding the thick oak door with her fist. "Hello, hello? Anyone there? Are you open?"

Obviously not. The door was locked, the shop was dark. Pansy pressed her forehead against the stained-glass panel, trying to see inside. Impossible through the thick colored glass. She went over to the narrow window, which was empty, blanked by the fly-specked shade pulled down inside it. There was a space of two inches at the bottom, though, and when she scraped the ice off the window and squinted through the narrow gap she could see that the shop hadn't yet been cleaned out.

Pansy went back to the door and started pounding again. Her voice rose. "Mademoiselle Grimaldi! Please open up—it's Pansy Kingsmith! Remember me?"

A young man in an orange Copy Copy vest came out of the building next door to gape at her. She'd made a spectacle of herself, which would have been a first if it wasn't for last night. "Hi," she said, offering him a weak, yes-I'm-sane smile. "Are you familiar with the business hours of this store?" She waved at the locked door. "I can't get inside."

The young man shivered and shoved his hands into his

pockets. "It's not open. Never *been* open. Not as long as I've been working at Copy Copy—going on two years, now."

Pansy let out a short huff of a laugh. "You're kidding."

"Occasionally we get people knocking, but clearly…" He gestured at the forlorn, abandoned storefront.

"They were having a Valentine's Day sale," Pansy insisted. "I saw the sign in the window just the other day. I went inside!" She rattled the latch.

The young man shrugged, stomping his feet on the frosty sidewalk. "Good luck," he said, and went back inside the copy store, casting a wary look at her over his shoulder.

Trying to maintain her cool because he was keeping an eye on her through Copy Copy's windows, Pansy knocked once more. "Mademoiselle Grimaldi?" she called softly. Regardless of the young man's apparent lack of observational skills, she was certain that the love potion shop and its exotic proprietor were real. They had to be.

The door opened a crack. Mademoiselle Grimaldi's face appeared in the gap, caked with heavy makeup: a slash of peacock blue on each eyelid, orangey tan rouge, scarlet lips. "No returns," she said, and started to close the door.

"I don't want my money back." Pansy grabbed the latch. "I need—" *Did she really?* "—an antidote."

The shopkeeper shook her head, which was wrapped in a bulbous black velvet turban. "No antidotes."

"Advice, then?" Pansy said, pushing politely but insistently at the door. "Please? There's been a, er, mistake."

The other woman stolidly blocked the way inside. "Mademoiselle Grimaldi never make mistake."

"No, but Pansy Kingsmith does."

"*Phht.*" Mademoiselle Grimaldi pressed a plump hand to the neckline of her draped black velvet robe. "Impossible. Love philtre is infallible."

Pansy clutched the brass latch. "The wrong man—"

"Wrong man is right man." Mademoiselle Grimaldi made a shooing gesture. "Now go 'way."

"You have to help me...."

"Wrong man is right man. He waits for you. Go home."

"Not until you tell me—ouch!" A flash of heat shot through the brass door latch. Pansy yelped and hopped backward on the sidewalk, holding out her scorched palm. The door slammed shut.

She rocked back on her heels. "How did you do that?" she whimpered, then, catching the curious eye of the copy store employee, she waved goodbye with her throbbing hand and trotted down Nitschke Street as fast as she dared without looking like an escapee from the loony bin.

Jane Kenton was waiting in her car at the corner. She'd refused to visit Mademoiselle Grimaldi's shop on the grounds that Pansy was only digging herself a deeper hole. "Did you see that?" Pansy said breathlessly, piling into the car. She held out her hand. "I think it's burned."

Jane shook her head. "What are you talking about? I see a small red mark, but that's all I see."

"Weren't you watching?" Pansy demanded. She touched her palm and flinched. "*Ow.* At least tell me you got a glimpse of Mademoiselle Grimaldi."

"I saw you pounding on the door of a closed shop...."

"She opened the door—just a crack. I talked to her."

Jane looked supercilious; because of her long, narrow nose and scholarly glasses, she was very good at it.

"I'm not making this up," Pansy said hotly. She felt like a kid with an invisible friend. "You've seen the love potion, anyway. That's something."

"Whatever." Jane sniffed. "Well, did you get an antidote?"

Pansy exhaled. "No."

"So...?"

"Mademoiselle Grimaldi doesn't believe a mistake was made," Pansy admitted in a low voice.

Jane smiled loftily and tapped her fingers on the steering wheel. "There's a thought."

Pansy pouted. "It figures you'd say that."

"It seems to me—"

"Yeah, yeah, I know."

Jane went on stubbornly. "You were in heaven until you found out his name. What does that tell you?"

"Still," Pansy said, equally stubborn, "I thought he was Jesse. And he knows I thought he was Jesse." She threw up her hands. "And then there's Jesse. How come *he* bathed in the love potion but wasn't drawn to me the way Peter was?"

"The other girl in the hot tub might have had something to do with it," Jane said dryly.

"Jesse was supposed to be bound to me for a lifetime. Or at least for Valentine's Day." The thought of spending Valentine's Day without Jesse—and Peter had no business being a part of her desire—made Pansy miserable. "Oh, Jane, I'm so mixed up. What do I do now?"

"It seems obvious to me."

"Do you have to be so darn *rational* all the time?"

"You were, once." Jane started the car. "Quit complaining and take a clear look at the situation, Pansy. Lots of women would love to have a man like Peter Angelini show up on their doorstep with his heart in his hand. It doesn't matter what put him there."

His heart in his hand. Pansy stroked her reddened palm, wondering if Jane knew what she was talking about. Were Peter's feelings for her real? Was he the right "wrong" man?

IN THE TWO DAYS since the love potion fiasco, Pansy had quit watching Jesse's six o'clock sports report. His handsome face, in a way now all too familiar, mocked her.

Unfortunately, this gave her way too much time to think. And since she didn't dare think about making love with Peter—even though her body, simmering with striking, tactile memories and unresolved longings, served as a constant reminder of that which was too good to forget—she had to think about the *situation*. And all the reasons she'd gotten herself into it. She'd come to a few startling conclusions.

Friday was Valentine's Day; Pansy did her best to ignore it. She came home late from work and clomped up the steps without stopping to visit with Mr. Barney. He'd given her a sweet, old-fashioned valentine that morning and dotingly invited her over for hot chocolate after work. When she'd hemmed and hawed, Mr. Barney had blustered something about a pretty young girl like her having a date, of course. But she had seen by the sympathetic look in his eyes that he suspected otherwise.

Pansy let herself into her apartment. "Hey, Tux," she said, her voice as heavy as the book bag she hung on the closet doorknob. She kicked off her boots and hung up her coat, tired of cold, tired of snow, tired of winter. Tired of herself and her mixed-up emotions.

"Tux?" She frowned at the shadowy apartment, noticing with half a mind that she'd left a light on in the bathroom. She was mainly wondering about Tux. He was a courteous cat; unless he'd found a patch of irresistible sunshine, he usually greeted her at the door. Worried, she hit the lights.

No Tux. But there was a trail of red rose petals that led from the entryway to the dining table and then looped around to the partially open bathroom door on the other side of the large room. Pansy was dumbstruck.

Who...?

Carefully she followed the scattered petals to the table in the dormer with the balcony doors. It was already dark outside, dark and frigid, but inside it was warm. And getting warmer deep inside *her* as she picked up the glass of red wine, the single long-stemmed red rose and the glittering red valentine that had been left on the pine table. The valentine was preprinted with the usual "Be Mine" message, but underneath that was handwritten: "Bathe yourself in luxury...."

"Is someone here?" Pansy said in a shaky, high-pitched voice. The apartment felt empty, but that didn't stop her wild imagination from conjuring up a handsome, brown-haired, blue-eyed man in a tuxedo. He beckoned. She took a sip of the wine and followed the trail of rose petals to the bathroom.

The two candlestick lamps that were fixed on either side of the mirror had been lit, the dancing flames making the ruby glass bead shades glow with rosy light. Her old boat of a bathtub was filled to the brim with an extravagantly sudsy bubble bath.

Pansy dipped a hand into the water. Warm. Nearly hot. "Tux, honey," she said, "did you run me a bath?" The cat, sitting complacently on the commode, slowly blinked his all-knowing green eyes and didn't answer. Instead he cocked his head and began fastidiously licking a paw. Tied around his neck was a red ribbon that looked a little the worse for wear.

Pansy laughed.

She looked at the card again and shrugged. "Bathe yourself in luxury," she said lightly, putting down the wineglass to unzip her skirt.

She lolled in the bath for a good twenty minutes, waiting for something else to happen. When nothing did, save the water turning tepid and her wineglass going dry, she idly concerned herself with the bud vase that had been left beside the bathtub. Suspicion sharpening, she picked it up to examine it more closely. Another single red rose had been stuck through the narrow neck, but when she took out the flower the bud vase looked a lot like a ruby red version of the glass vial that had held the Angel Water. She sniffed at the heavy, cloying sweetness that still clung to the inside of the red vial. And suddenly she shuddered at the slippery touch of the sweet, silken bathwater she'd been so enjoying.

Coincidence? She thought not.

A strange, tingling sensation began to prickle through her bloodstream. It crept over her skin like a horde of tiny spiders. The short hairs at her nape and on her forearms rose, whether in apprehension or arousal, Pansy wasn't sure. She gripped the edge of the tub.

"Get ahold of yourself, girl," she whispered. "You're jumping to conclusions." The card had read "Bathe yourself in luxury," *not* "Bathe yourself in a love potion and, by the way, welcome to your comeuppance!"

Still…

With another delicate shudder, she rose from the bath, quickly dried herself and put on a thick, comfy terry-cloth robe. She started brushing her hair, then stopped suddenly to focus on the stirrings of her body. Did she feel a strange craving? Was she getting any overwhelming desires?

Make that any *new* ones?

"Nonsense," she said, stepping into the other room. "I no longer believe in love potions." She looked up at Tux's plaintive meow and stopped dead in her tracks.

Two brown-haired, blue-eyed men in tuxedos stood in the center of her attic apartment. Two men almost exactly alike. They looked at her and smiled and said in perfect unison, "Pick your valentine, Pansy Kingsmith."

9

In dreams, let me my true love see

PETER THOUGHT PANSY was going to faint. She opened and closed her mouth several times. She passed a hand over her eyes and clutched at her hair and shook her head. She wavered, her bare toes clenching at the rag rug as if gravity was no longer reliable. Finally she drew a deep breath, gathered herself together and looked them over from head to wingtip with narrowed eyes.

Pete held on to the agate in his pocket so tightly his fingers began to cramp.

And then, miracle of miracles, Pansy walked straight over to him. *To him.*

Pete barely noticed Jesse's sigh of relief and quick escape. He was thinking only that Pansy's smile was the most wonderful thing he'd ever seen. Sweet as a chocolate bar. Warm as July. Dizzying as a merry-go-round because it was really, truly aimed at *him*, Peter Angelini.

She tossed her head, trying to appear saucy. "So, which one are you—Jesse or Peter?"

"I think you know."

"Lately, I'm not so sure of anything," she said in a much softer voice.

"Peter Angelini." He put out his hand. "Pleased to make your acquaintance."

She tucked her hands behind her back and murmured something indistinguishable, shyly swinging her face aside.

"For future reference, note that my hair is slightly longer than Jesse's. Sometimes ragged. I don't get it cut as often as I should and I don't have a close, personal relationship with my hair dryer."

Pansy's lashes flickered. "I can tell you apart. For one, Jesse's so brown."

"It's supposed to be a secret, but…" Pete put his hand to his mouth and whispered, "He goes to a tanning salon."

Her small laugh was tremulous. "You have a crooked tooth. And you're about ten pounds lighter."

He flexed his biceps. "Not so much muscle mass."

Pansy's throat closed. She hadn't noticed any lack when they'd— But she wasn't supposed to think about that. Funny how her mind was suddenly filling with potent images, renewing the prickle of electric desires that had swept through her in the bathtub. If Peter had doused her with a love potion, it was working something fierce.

"I don't wear designer labels," he said.

She didn't care. "Your eyes are bluer."

"Really?" He scrunched his forehead in a way that she was already coming to think of as entirely Peter. "Are you sure?"

"Definitely." Why hadn't she seen all these differences before? Or was it possible that she had…intuitively? "You have a small birthmark," she added shyly, thinking of the not entirely kosher way she'd discovered his most personal identifying marks. "And a scar on your elbow."

"Noticed that, did you?"

Her face was hot. "I'm very observant."

Peter shrugged. "All in all, I'm the scaled-down, plainfolks version of my older twin. Less glamorous, more dependable."

"I wouldn't necessarily say that." She'd automatically leapt to Peter's defense, surprising herself. Not for a moment had she thought of him as a lesser version. Only different, and not the twin she'd been set on. Now, though, having had time to think about it...

"You'd have reason," he admitted, misinterpreting her. His brow puckered as he put out his hand. "I'm sorry, Pansy. I misled you, and it was a rotten thing to do. There's no excuse, but I'm still hoping you can forgive me, because..." He took a deep breath. "Because even though I was with you under false pretenses the other night, nothing that I said to you was a lie."

Pansy saw sincerity in his eyes—and the flame of an attraction still so powerful she knew that any contact at all could incinerate them both. Still, she had to take the hand he offered, or he'd think her rude and inflexible. And she was nothing if not polite.

She put out her hand; their fingertips touched. "I..."

Peter's palm slid against hers with a comforting ease. Enveloped in warmth, she sighed as he drew her closer. *Coming home.* Just like coming home.

If she followed her heart instead of her head, what would happen? Another disaster? Or was it possible that she'd never have to lose this sense of perfect fulfillment?

Standing close, her fingers knotted with his, Pansy lifted her face in an unspoken invitation. She'd tried the same move with Jesse after their second date and he hadn't picked up on it. Obviously by intention.

Peter chose differently. He lowered his mouth to hers and kissed her, gently at first, as befitted their tentative rapprochement. It didn't take long before the heat started to rise between them, the soft touch of his lips led to the warm thrust of his tongue. With languid skill, he kissed her deeply and thoroughly, pressing their clasped hands between her breasts in a gesture that was as much a promise as a caress.

Pansy squeezed his hand, the tenderness of her burned palm a fitting reminder that there were things in the world that she couldn't hope to understand or control—magical, mystical, marvelous things.

And feelings she didn't *want* to understand or control—passionate, tempestuous feelings that were to be experienced, not analyzed with a level head and a rule book.

At that, she kissed him with her mouth open, parting her robe at the same time and moving his hand over to her breast. He moaned in his need, pressing himself into her, his fingers finding her nipple and doing delicious things to it as she let the robe slide away.

"Very nice," he said, squeezing her, hugging her, laughing into her hair. "My valentine."

Joy surged in Pansy. She felt free enough to break from his arms and hop onto the bed and sit there with her arms open, offering him her heart in her hands. Pete's moves were smoother than James Bond's as he shed the tuxedo in record time, and then for many delirious minutes it was just them together, naked, grateful, reverent, loving.

When finally he slid slowly inside her, filling her, bringing her home, she opened her eyes to his and whispered, "Nice to meet you, Peter Angelini."

He rocked deeper into her, the rich, sweet passion of it thickening his voice. "The pleasure's all mine, Pansy Kingsmith."

AFTER THEY'D MADE LOVE and laughed quite giddily at their unmanageable attraction for each other; after they'd had wine and cheese and crackers in bed and finally gotten around to talking about themselves, their words tumbling over each other in a kind of haphazard race to overdue emotional intimacy even though Pete already seemed uncannily to know so much about Pansy and she about him; after Tux had made a bed on Pete's discarded trousers—a sure sign of approval—she began to explain what she had realized about herself over the past few days.

Jesse—not the family man she'd made up in her daydreams, but the *real* Jesse—was not her heart's desire, after all. Whatever the impact of the Angel Water and the agate, she had nonetheless been detoured to the right man.

"My fantasy had nothing to do with Jesse," she confessed. "Well, superficially, maybe, because I did think he was attractive. The problem was that I imagined him as the perfect husband, and that's just not Jesse, is it? I pictured us as a family, living happily ever after in the ideal Victorian house, stringing popcorn for the Christmas tree and going to church on Sunday and barbecuing on the deck with the kids splashing nearby in a wading pool."

"No hot tub?" Pete asked with uplifted brows, his chin resting on Pansy's crown. She was nestled against him in the pine four-poster bed, as comfortably as if she'd been made to fit his body.

She chuckled. "The hot tub's for the parents...after the children are in bed."

"It sounds like a nice dream. Maybe we can make it come true."

She turned to look at him, alarmed. "I can't imagine being so impulsive, not after...well, you know."

"Oh, I'm not asking you to marry me." Pete paused for a beat, then grinned. "Not yet, anyway."

Pansy nodded solemnly enough, but her face had been set aglow. It was confounding and illogical and much too sudden, but Pete knew, and he knew that Pansy knew, that they were meant to be together. Because although Pete may have *looked* like Jesse, he was another man entirely.

"IT'S A SHAME ABOUT Jesse selling the house." Pansy sighed with longing. "It is perfect."

"Jesse and I might be able to work out a deal," Pete said, thinking that his bachelor-pad condo was more his brother's style anyway—unless Jesse's sudden, powerful attraction to Claudia was actually going to last. "Because I do like that hot tub. Maybe there *was* something in the water...."

Dimpling, Pansy pressed her lips together to contain her smile. She looked at their hands entwined on the pillow and decided to keep her secret. Unless... "Pete? About that bubble bath you drew for me. Was there something you wanted to confess?"

He was silent for a long while before he chuckled lazily. "Well, as it happens, it's an unusual story. Perhaps one you'd recognize. You see, I was going to the copy place on Nitschke Street when I saw an odd sign in the window of a strange little shop. It wasn't the kind of place I'd normally frequent, but something seemed to draw me inside...."

Heart's Desire

If you could be anyone you wanted to be—fabulous
heiress, adventuress, enchantress…
If you could have the lover of a lifetime give you his
heart in a valentine…
But that only happens in fairy tales…doesn't it?

1

ANGIE DUBONNET SWAYED in sync with the chandelier as the cruise ship pitched in the turbulent sea. She was nearly desperate enough to blame her queasy feeling on seasickness so she'd have reason to gracefully bow out of the rest of the extravagant multicourse meal. One of the newlywed brides at the table for eight did stagger to her feet—*ungracefully*—a napkin pressed to her mouth. Her husband muttered an apology and escorted her from the dining room.

"Hold on to me, sweetheart," said Trent Irving, Angie's self-appointed dinner companion. Leering, he seized the opportunity to lunge at her, but lost his balance when the ship plowed into another wave. Instead of putting his arm around her, he slammed his elbow between her shoulder blades.

"Oof!" Angie exhaled at the sharp stab of pain. She gritted her teeth. *He's trying to be considerate*, she told herself. Trent couldn't know that his slick smile and sleazy touch made her stomach turn somersaults.

Trent righted himself. "Sorry," he breathed hotly in her ear, clamping his clammy hand on her bare shoulder.

Angie suppressed a shudder. "That's okay." She was trying to unobtrusively shrug out from under his hold when the dining room canted sickeningly off-kilter once more, causing their dinner plates to slide across the round table. Silverware rattled; overhead, the crystal teardrops of the chandelier clicked like chips in the shipboard casino.

Angie rescued her sloshing wineglass and the basket of dinner rolls, nudging her untouched plate of grilled snapper away from the table edge with the back of her hand. "I'm fine, Trent. Really. You can let go now."

He leaned closer, squeezing tighter. "I know how you gals like a strong shoulder to lean on."

"I'm *fine.*"

"You are that." He licked his lips. She blanched, the stench of his cologne making her eyes tear.

"I never get seasick," she insisted, as if she'd had extensive experience on the open sea. "But I'm afraid you don't look so good." Up close, Trent's Florida tan was more orange than bronze, with a sallow green undertone. "Maybe you should—"

"Yee-haw!" someone called as the ship seesawed yet again. The floor tilted precariously. Cries of alarm went up all over the room as crystal and silver tumbled to the carpet. Several people jumped up wearing their uneaten food on their new clothes. Waiters staggered between the tables with sponges and napkins, setting things to right.

The crowd thinned considerably as another round of unsteady diners made for the exits. "You should go to the infirmary," Angie told Trent as she slid out from under his clinging arm. "You're as green as the Lucky Charms leprechaun."

He swallowed thickly. "Lucky Charms?"

The ship swayed again, less violently. Angie gripped the back of the chair adjacent to her own; it had remained empty throughout the dinner service. "It's a kids' cereal," she explained. "With marshmallow cutouts shaped like— oh, never mind."

Angie didn't want to get into anything that had to do with her job as a nursery-school teacher; this Caribbean cruise was her long-awaited vacation from all that. When her tablemates had introduced themselves—two pairs of honeymooners, a newly divorced, stockily built beauti-

cian from Pittsburgh, and Trent Irving, Miami car salesman and would-be Romeo—Angie had given her name
but avoided other details. She'd left the workaday Angie
Dubonnet behind in Maple Hills, Michigan, fast-frozen in
a snowdrift for the length of this seven-day luxury cruise.
She hadn't scrimped and saved for three years just to
have the same conversations with the same type of people
she knew back home.

Trent seemed determined to stay with her despite his
obvious reaction to the tossing ship. "I'll escort you back
to your room," he said, lurching to his feet.

Angie waved him off. "I'm going out on deck for a
breath of fresh air." She smiled brightly. "I don't mind
that the waves are going up—" Trent paled as he followed the course of her swooping hand "—and down like
a roller coaster."

He sank back into his seat, his devotion suddenly
soured. When the divorcée began to outline her surefire
remedy for seasickness to the depleted table, Angie
grabbed her clutch purse off the wine-stained tablecloth
and made her escape.

Walking unsteadily—as much a result of her unaccus-
tomed high heels as the motion of the ship—she crossed
the blue-and-gold dining room and climbed the staircase
to the promenade deck. This wasn't how she'd imagined
her first evening aboard ship. By all rights, she should
have met a handsome, debonair stranger by now and be
leaning with him against the railing, basking in the glow
of a full moon, a million stars and a thrilling shipboard romance.

Instead she had Trent Irving, who was handsome
enough if you didn't mind hair oil and capped teeth, and
a murky sea so rough it threatened to pitch her headfirst
over the railing. She gripped the top rail tightly and
sighed. Was it too much to ask for a little bit of seaborne
enchantment?

Charcoal gray clouds had blotted out the stars. The growl of distant thunder foretold an impending rain shower. Angie didn't want to give up and retire to her cabin so soon, even though the wind-whipped salt spray was already doing nasty things to her silk dress. The dress was brand-new, too, expensive and spaghetti-strapped, sinfully skimpy, patterned with a floral design bright enough to detract from skin so pale it fairly shouted, "I haven't seen the sun in three-and-a-half months."

Better white than green, Angie decided as the cruise ship plowed through another set of wicked waves. She trained her eyes on the horizon, looking for the smudgy blur that was Florida. The churning in her stomach subsided. For a landlubber, she was doing okay. It would take more than a February storm at sea and a disappointing seating assignment to knock *her* off course.

Angie was determined to enjoy this cruise even if it killed her.

Not that the situation was as dire as all that. At least she was away from Trent and still on her wobbly high heels—which was unfortunately the best she could say for her vacation thus far. When she'd emptied her savings account to purchase the cruise ticket, her main objective had been sun-splashed relaxation. But she wouldn't say no if an opportunity for a shipboard fling presented itself. She'd watched *Love Boat*; she knew how these things went.

Or were supposed to. Boarding in Miami, Angie had soon realized that the *Sea Siren*'s valentine cruise was not quite the venue for romance that she'd hoped for. Drawn by the holiday theme, couples abounded—newlyweds, mainly, but also young lovers, old lovers and frazzled in-between lovers with rambunctious kids in tow. Then there were the seniors—scads of sprightly ladies in discount-fare groups, a sprinkling of silver-haired gents in cranberry slacks and gleaming white belts that matched their dentures, and a whole host of firmly fixed, well-to-do couples flaunting their diamonds, money clips and upper-deck staterooms. Aside from a boisterous college tour group, the remaining handful of singles, most of them female, had eyed each other with sinking hopes as they negotiated the embarkation ritual.

Contemplatively, Angie looked out over the water. She would enjoy herself anyway. There were still the sumptuous buffets, endless entertainments and island excursions, and—unless this storm developed into a typhoon—lots of sea and sand and sun. Finding a fantasy lover would be merely the icing on the cake.

Though the heavy gray clouds hadn't dissipated, the wind seemed to be dying down. The sea was less rough, laced only now and then by the deadly whitecaps. Angie closed her eyes and breathed deeply of the humid salt air, calculating how many minutes she had before Trent Irving recovered his sea legs and came to find her.

She didn't mean to be unkind to Trent. His attention was flattering, she supposed, considering the ratio of suitable single men to women on board. He just wasn't what she'd wished for all those evenings when she'd worked night shift at the minimart to earn extra cash. Plane tickets, a new wardrobe that included her first formal gown since prom, sunglasses, sunscreen and other sundries, and, of course, the Caribbean cruise of a lifetime did not come cheap.

Under the circumstances, she felt justified in setting her sights higher than the Trent Irvings of the world.

She did date; she'd even had a couple of relationships with very nice men...who'd ultimately bored her to tears. Because although she wanted a loving, stable marriage, she couldn't help also wanting a different sort of man—someone exciting, exotic, unpredictable. A man who would thrill her.

But, darn it, she just wasn't the type of woman cruise-ship dreamboats were drawn to!

Her problem was that she was still only Angie Dubon-net—beloved nursery school teacher, doting mother to two overfed cats, gardener, knitter, cyclist and mortgage-holder. She had straight brown hair and hazel eyes and a body that made a perfect lap to cuddle toddlers on at story time.

Angie tilted back her head and drew in a deep breath of the intoxicating sea air. *If only she could become someone other than reliable, dependable Angie Dubonnet for the length of the valentine voyage...*

A movement farther along the deck distracted Angie from her thoughts. She gave a tiny gasp as a man emerged from one of the stairwells and stepped over to the railing. Now, then! *He,* she thought with a tingling attraction, was everything a fantasy man should be. It was almost as if the gods had read her mind all those long winter evenings when she'd devoured glitzy, sexy paper-back romances behind the counter at the minimart, daring herself to become her own heroine by injecting a shot of excitement into her withering love life.

Fate had just done the job for her. The fantasy man was fairly tall, with wavy black hair and a lithe, muscular frame perfect for showing off his tailored smoky-blue suit and pearl gray silk shirt and tie. He was handsome, too, from what she could tell at a distance, but not so drop-dead gorgeous that he seemed entirely out of her reach.

Angie fixed her flapping skirt. *Tall, dark and handsome.* Who could ask for anything more?

Not her. And while back home she probably wouldn't have dared to approach a complete stranger, this cruise ship was not in any way similar to her normal environment. She tipped up her chin and sucked in her stomach. No reason she couldn't at least stroll his way and see what happened.

Angie walked slowly down the promenade deck, trailing her fingertips along the railing for balance. The man glanced at her and smiled a smile that hit her at the back of her knees like a karate chop. She faltered, but kept on going.

He took a step toward her, his eyes lighting up. Angie thrilled. At the same moment another woman came up from below deck, calling the stranger's name, holding two champagne glasses and laughing delightedly at his surprise as he turned to greet her. Nikolas, she called him.

Angie halted abruptly. Disappointment lodged itself like a heavy stone in the pit of her stomach. She turned on her heel, slipping on the wet deck just enough to make her grab the railing for support. Glancing back, she saw that the glamorous couple were too absorbed in each other to notice her clumsiness.

The woman was of a type that intimidated Angie. Wealth and confidence oozed from every pore. Her corn-silk-blond hair was arranged in an artful swirl, with cunning tendrils curling against her swanlike neck. She was slender as a wand except for the generous breasts spilling from a liquid silver strapless gown, and not only did she float like a fairy in her strappy silver sandals, she apparently knew exactly what to whisper in a man's ear to make him flush with desire.

Biting her lip, Angie turned away to face the vast expanse of dark water, letting the salt spray cool her hot face. Her dreams of a fantasy man were hopeless. Even if he did appear, she could never live up to her part of the scenario.

She stepped away from the railing, glancing once more at the lovers before lowering herself into one of the deck chairs roped down in the shadows. *Face it,* she told herself. *You could never be like that woman.*

Or could she?

The couple put their heads together and murmured intimately before moving on, passing within spitting distance of Angie's chair. She ducked her head, hugging herself in the sheltering darkness as fat raindrops began to splatter the deck.

Could she?

Dare she?

She was on vacation, after all. Not a soul on board knew anything about her except for her name, and even that could be altered. She could make herself over into a character from one of her books. Heck, she'd already splurged on the extravagant new wardrobe. All she needed was the courage. The audacity.

Angie's eyes widened. Well…why not?

She didn't have to be Angie Dubonnet, responsible citizen. She could be Angelique Dubonnet, fun-loving heiress, adventurous world traveler. Sexy, free, vivacious. The belle of the ship.

Angelique Dubonnet—enchantress.

2

THE STORM HAD PASSED by the next morning. Angie leapt from her bed and peered out the porthole in her tiny cabin, more than ready for the cruise she'd dreamed of to begin. The Caribbean sky was a brilliant azure, nearly cloudless, and the ocean made blue satin ripples as far as the eye could see. Sunshine glittered on the water. It was a perfect day to launch the *USS Angelique Dubonnet*.

After a quick shower, she scanned the day's itinerary that had been slipped under her door, looking for activities that would suit Angelique. Bingo, shuffleboard, bridge? Not on her charmed life. Aerobic classes? Probably a good idea, but…sweaty. Trapshooting? Maybe, if she was such a great markswoman all the men would be awed by her prowess. As Angie was a sharpshooter only with a water pistol, trapshooting was out. *The Horse Whisperer* was showing in the cinema, which would do only if Angelique had an escort to whisper sweet nothings in *her* ear….

She decided to take the morning to work on her transformation into a femme fatale. She'd graze the lunch buffet, then secure a spot on one of the early afternoon tours of Nassau's historical sites. Maybe afterward she'd try out her new persona on the beaches before making the really big plunge—Angelique's grand entrance at dinner.

By five o'clock Angie was seated in the shade beneath a thatch-roofed, open-air seaside café. Aside from an inevitable sunburn, her playacting was going surprisingly well. Sunning on a white sand beach, she'd struck up an acquaintance with several Japanese tourists who'd obligingly nodded and smiled at Angie's—or rather *Angelique's*—discourse on the merits of various famous beaches around the world. Thank heaven Angie had always liked glitzy life-styles-of-the-rich-and-decadent beach books; she'd sounded fairly knowledgeable when she'd assured the Japanese that there wasn't a beach to rival the Côte d'Azur.

Two elderly ladies approached Angie's table with hopeful smiles and exotic drinks sporting paper parasols. "May we sit with you, dear?" one of them asked, putting down a souvenir-stuffed bag bearing the gold-and-blue cruise ship logo. "Every other place seems to be taken."

Angie stretched out a graceful hand. "Please be my guests," she said lazily. The ladies might be fellow passengers from the *Sea Siren,* but they looked harmless enough in their native straw hats and brightly colored cruise wear. She could safely practice her Angelique on them.

"I'm Angelique Dubonnet," she said, giving the name her best high-school French pronunciation. She slid her sunglasses up her forehead and squinted at them. "Are you both from the cruise ship?"

"Yes, indeed," said one of the ladies. She had a firm manner, strawberry blond hair and lots of freckles that merged with age spots to mottle her pale skin. "My name is Virginia Neill, and that's Victoria."

"Vicki," said Victoria, who, in a neon cartoon T-shirt and walking shorts, looked like the more spirited of the pair. "We're sisters from Seattle, Washington. Are you French?"

"Not exactly." Angie knew she couldn't pull *that* off. "But I spend a lot of time there, at my villa in Provence." Good thing she'd also read a lot of travel books.

"Lucky girl," Vicki said. She took off her straw hat, revealing a pouf of slightly compressed, pink-tinged hair identical to her sister's. "Ooh, I'd love to visit the south of France. Can't we go, Virgie?"

"Perhaps next year."

"I've always enjoyed it." Smiling, Angie bent her head over the straw of her icy green island punch. "The Côte d'Azur is smashing good fun."

Vicki looked interested, but Virginia frowned. "Topless bathing." She smoothed her pristine red-and-white-striped middy blouse. "Not for us, sister."

Vicki sipped from a lavishly garnished coconut shell. "When in Rome…" She giggled. "Or should I say, when in France…"

"Yes, it's true." Angie tried to look blasé. "Everyone does it." She couldn't imagine frolicking on a topless beach, but she was sure that Angelique would. With madcap abandon.

"You make such a pretty picture, sitting there in that dress the color of the sea," confided Vicki. "Virgie and I wondered if we should disturb you." Her eyes danced. "I thought you might be rendezvousing with a young man—a shipboard fling, perhaps…?"

"Vicki, really," her sister said repressively.

Angie smiled mysteriously, thinking of Mr. Tall, Dark and Handsome from the past evening. He should be so fortunate. Obviously the manicure, pedicure and chic new haircut she'd splurged on at the shipboard salon had been a wise investment. Even the aqua, halter-top sundress, purchased at a price equal to several days' pay, had been worth every penny. Now if only she could use them to knock the socks off her elusive shipboard fling!

"Actually," she confided with a just-us-girls lift of the brows, "I'm between lovers at the moment."

Vicki's eyes popped. "Between lovers! You *lucky* girl."

"I'm on my way to join a sunken-treasure expedition," Angie said extravagantly. "This cruise is only a pit stop for me. I was climbing mountains in Italy, and I needed a brief rest before diving for gold in a shipwreck just discovered off Bimini."

"I should say!"

"I hope we're finished in time for carnival in Rio." Angie tossed her glossy head. Her imagination billowed like a hot air balloon, tethered only by Virginia's dubious regard; Vicki was the perfect audience.

Virginia screwed up her nose. "More topless shenanigans."

"The dancers are rather provocative," Angie agreed, sharing a smug smile with Vicki.

"Ooh," the enthusiastic younger sister sighed. "I wish—"

Virginia slapped the straw hat back on Vicki's head. "We must get back to the ship. We want to leave plenty of time to dress for the captain's cocktail party."

Vicki sucked up the dregs of her tiki hurricane and rose with reluctance. "We'll see you there, I imagine, Angelique?"

Angie blinked, but held her smile. Apparently she'd misjudged the sisters. Only important personages were invited to be the captain's guests. Vicki and Virginia must be part of the upper-deck crowd.

"Umm…" Angie pretended to be considering an array of choices. "Perhaps," she said airily. "I really haven't decided."

"Do come!" Vicki urged as her sister took her elbow and towed her toward the exit. "You know how stuffy these cocktail parties can be. We need a lively young person like you to get things going."

"I'll try." Angie kept smiling until the sisters had cleared the café. Then she let her shoulders slump. Of course Angelique Dubonnet would be the captain's guest. A woman like her wouldn't be caught dead dining with an oily haired car salesman, two pairs of googly-eyed newlyweds and a beautician determined to blow her divorce settlement on blackjack.

AFTER TAKING A TAXI back to the docked ship, Angie lingered on one of the upper decks instead of returning to her claustrophobic cabin. One deck down, she could hear a calypso band playing near the outdoor pool. The cheerful music stirred her blood. She wanted to kick up her heels and dance—even if it was only with Trent Irving.

Maybe creating the Angelique character hadn't been such a great idea. She'd managed to bluff her way through it so far, but it wouldn't take much to plunge her beyond her depth.

There was still time to give it up, with no harm done. She could manage to enjoy the cruise even if it didn't meet all her romantic expectations.

Angie closed her eyes and basked in the warm breeze blowing across the busy harbor. Should she bail out before the USS Angelique sank to the bottom of the Caribbean?

"Angelique," someone called from behind her. "Oh, Angelique!"

Angie's smile was instantaneous. "Vicki," she said warmly, forgetting to be Angelique as she turned to welcome her new friend.

Vicki waved. "Look who I've brought to meet you!"

Angie's eyes went round as marbles. Walking toward her was the man from last night, the dreamboat with the glamorous girlfriend. He was even more handsome than she remembered, very appealing in crisp khaki shorts and a white shirt that was blinding against the bronze of his tan. Desire hit her with a wallop, blasting away all thoughts of quitting her charade.

"I just know you two will hit it off," Vicki exclaimed as they approached. She gave a little hop and skip, jogging the arm of her companion in enthusiasm.

The dark-eyed stranger stopped before Angie and re-
garded her with obvious appreciation. Aware that the
wind was molding her filmy aqua dress against her body,
she struggled to refrain from crossing her arms in front of
herself like a bashful schoolgirl. Angelique types flaunted
their bodies. Of course, they had personal-trainer-toned
figures that were eminently flauntable.

Angie's cheeks were already sun flushed; under the
dreamboat's gaze she felt them growing warmer yet. It
took an act of supreme strength to summon up an Angelique attitude when her heart was drumming out of her
chest. Very coolly, she extended her hand.

"Angelique, may I present Nikolas Dorian," Vicki said.
She bounced beneath her straw hat. "Niko, this is Angelique Dubonnet. Isn't she a cutie pie? You must help me to
convince her to attend the captain's cocktail party."

Nikolas Dorian took Angie's hand and grazed the top
of it with a whisper of a kiss. Her fingers curled into his,
tightening involuntarily. "Mr. Dorian," she said.

"Call me Niko."

He kept her hand. Heat flared in places other than Angie's cheeks. "Niko," she agreed, the name spoken in a
husky whisper.

"Ooh, don't you two make a lovely couple?" cooed
Vicki. "Wait—I've just had a brilliant idea. Niko, you
should escort Angelique to the party. We'll have such fun
together!"

Vicki's exuberance was catching. Angie felt that she
could be Angelique. Why not? It would only be for five
more days. *And nights,* she silently added, studying
Niko's face from beneath her lowered lashes. He was
probably near her own age—early thirties—but there was
an expensive, well-groomed look about him that bespoke
luxury and privilege. There were no blemishes or scars to
detract from his good looks. His hair was a shade of black
so deep that it shone with blue highlights in the sunshine.

Below the tumble of short, glossy curls, his brow was noble, his eyes a velvety black, his nose and cleft chin strong and definitely masculine. A five o'clock shadow brought out the rosy hue of his firm mouth.

Angie melted inside. Nikolas was the type of virile man who'd have to shave before dinner, using lather and hot towels, slapping on an expensive aftershave that would seep into her pores like an aphrodisiac....

"It would be my pleasure to escort Angelique to the captain's party," he said, still holding her hand. He gave her fingers a playful squeeze. "What do you say, Angie? Want to pair up?"

She wondered briefly about last night's date, then dismissed the thought. In fact, Niko's casual air delighted her, as did the sparkle in his eyes. He wasn't the upper crust snob she'd halfway expected. Perhaps because her masquerade had turned her into one of "his kind."

But he'd called her Angie.

Only as an informality, she told herself, slipping her hand out of his even though she could easily imagine leaving it there for the remainder of the cruise. "Well, I..." She hesitated. Going as Niko's date would get her into the party with no questions asked. She should be jumping at the chance.

"Please say yes," urged Vicki. "I don't want to go if you don't go. I've had enough dull cocktail-party talk to last me a lifetime."

Angie nodded. "Since you put it that way..."

"Hurrah!" Vicki clapped her hands.

Niko made a short bow. "Ladies," he said, pecking Vicki's freckled cheek.

"Ooh," she breathed, simpering.

He raised his brows at Angie. "I'll see you at seven?"

She tried not to show her incredible excitement at the prospect. "Yes, at seven. I'm in—" Just in time she remembered that her tiny cabin, while not the least expensive available, was still not upper deck. "Why don't we meet in the Voyager's Lounge," she improvised, "and go on from there?"

"As you wish."

With identical mooning expressions, the two women watched Nikolas walk away. Then Vicki turned to Angie and said, in the age-old tradition, "What are you going to wear?"

As she discussed imaginary Galliano sheaths and backless Versace gowns, Angie thought only of Nikolas Dorian. He was almost certainly out of her league. But no one else knew that, so what did it matter?

Her conscience twinged. *Five days*, she thought. *Five nights*. The vacation of a lifetime.

The man of a hundred lifetimes.

"Tell me about Nikolas," she said to Vicki when the older woman paused in her monologue about whether the polka dots she adored were as passé as her sister claimed.

Vicki winked. "Isn't he yummy?"

Angelique or not, the only possible response was a girlish giggle and an enthusiastic nod. As the two women linked arms and began to stroll along the deck, Angie asked about the blonde who'd looked very cozy with Nikolas the night before. Vicki dismissed the other woman with a wave of her hand, swearing that Niko had confessed she wasn't his type, which was why Vicki had thought of Angelique. "You two seem made for each other."

From Angie's viewpoint, that was doubtful. But she didn't intend to reveal that fact, not when Nikolas Dorian was her best chance at fulfilling her vacation fantasy. "C'mon, Vicki." She bumped the older woman's hip. "Give me something to go on. Who is he?"

"No one quite seems to know," Vicki confided. "It's all very mysterious."

"I love a mystery," Angie declared.

Vicki nodded almost soberly as she talked. "Obviously he's a man of some importance. His manners and dress are impeccable, he's well-spoken and intelligent. Good breeding there, I'd say, but then the Hassenfusses from Philadelphia said that the Blankmores from Connecticut swear that there's a shady real-estate deal in his past, something to do with the EPA and swampland in Florida and a congressman in his back pocket. I forget exactly."

Angie blinked. "Really."

"I don't believe it myself." The brim of Vicki's hat bobbed in the breeze. "Because I was talking to the Cliftons from Atlanta this morning at breakfast and *they* said they knew a Nick Dorian who went to Yale with their son and he was a fine young man from an upstanding family. They thought he became an architect and moved to Chicago or Minneapolis or maybe Detroit—someplace cold, at any rate."

Angie bit her lip. Too close to home for comfort. "Is that so."

Vicki lowered her voice. "Personally, I think he's a descendant of poverty-stricken Greek fishermen who sailed to America and became millionaires. Don't you think Niko looks Greek?"

"Mmm, well, the name sounds Greek."

"Maybe Italian?"

"I couldn't say." Angie was beginning to think that Vicki had no idea what she was talking about, and that Nikolas Dorian was none of the above.

"Whatever the case, we can be sure he's handsome," Vicki concluded. She nudged Angie's side. "And seeing how you're between lovers—" Vicki chortled "—I couldn't resist a bit of matchmaking."

Angie felt herself blushing; there was no way to hide it.

"Color me thankful," she said with a laugh. *Very thankful,* she added silently, her optimism soaring higher than the gulls that wheeled across the brilliant sky. At last her dream vacation had begun.

3

NIKOLAS DORIAN SAT in a dark corner of the wood-paneled Voyager's Lounge. Brooding.

The woman, Angelique, was enchanting. He'd seen her on deck their first night at sea, her long hair blowing in the wind, her hips round and womanly in some sort of skimpy, flower-spattered thing that left her arms and shoulders bare. Her upturned face and pale-as-the-moon skin had beckoned to him in the darkness like a port in a storm.

He'd been all set to decline the captain's cocktail party when Vicki Neill had grabbed his arm and gone on and on about the divine young woman he absolutely must meet. Not having figured on the cruise being filled with so many elderly ladies who wanted to introduce him to so many eligible younger ladies, he'd wasted half his morning on the beach at Nassau making up a list of excuses to have at hand when he got back to the ship. Vicki had overridden all objections. And while she herself was sweet, she'd made this "delightful girl" of hers sound as bad as Raquel. He'd been avoiding the manhunter after a long evening of her rambling, champagne-fueled discourses on diets, fashions and favorite vacation spots.

But then Vicki had pointed out Angelique and he'd changed his mind about meeting her. Even with the new haircut, he'd recognized her. He did wonder, though— the girl he'd first noticed had looked rather frazzled at check-in, a winter coat slung over one arm. She hadn't seemed the sort to flit from scuba diving in Bimini to top-less dancing in Rio.

She'd shed that frazzled self along with the winter coat. She'd looked svelte and sophisticated and very self-possessed in her blue dress and high heels. The glossy mahogany wings of her hair had curved against her sun-kissed cheeks when she'd lowered her chin. He'd been dazzled when he caught her peeping up at him through her lashes, and had held on to her hand for longer than he'd meant to.

Although Vicki had rattled on about Cannes and Pro-vence, he'd placed Angelique's accent as strictly Upper Midwest. The chance that Angelique was playing games with her fellow passengers had intrigued him.

Nikolas thought that he might want to play out the cha-rade to see what would happen. And to see exactly how far she was willing to go....

As if his wish had conjured her up, Angelique walked into the nearly empty lounge. The heels on her golden sandals were ridiculously steep, but they did something quite magnificent to the expanse of leg that showed through the slit in her calf-length white dress. As she tripped over to his table, Nikolas stood to wolfishly ad-mire every flash of creamy leg the deep slit allowed. He was a lucky man—the slit went all the way up to one pro-vocatively lush thigh.

He murmured a greeting, kissed Angelique's soft cheek and settled her at the table. "Why don't we have a drink here before we go on to the party?"

"Sure," she said. "I'll have a, ah—"

"A champagne cocktail? That's what they'll be serving at the captain's shindig, so if you don't want to mix drinks…"

She smiled, nodded. "Yes, that will be fine. Thank you."

He went to get their drinks himself, because the return

trip would allow him another glimpse of her legs, now crossed beneath the table.

"How do you know Vicki?" he asked when he returned.

Angelique touched the stem of her glass with a shiny plum-colored nail. "I don't, really. We met in a café only this afternoon."

"Then you don't know who she is."

Angelique leaned back in her chair. "Not just a sweet little old lady from Seattle, I take it?"

"She's one of Daddy's Girls."

"Daddy's girls—?"

"The baked goods company. Daddy's Girls doughnuts. Daddy's Girls pies. Daddy's Girls cookies and crackers and devil's food cupcakes—"

Angelique laughed. "I get it."

"You've probably never tasted their stuff even though every grocery and convenience store in the country stocks it."

She shifted uneasily and raised her glass. "You'd be surprised."

Nikolas clasped his hands atop the table. "Tell me about yourself, Angelique."

Her laugh was as effervescent as her champagne cocktail. "Oh, Niko, please. It's so boring to talk about myself."

"Tell me just one thing, then," he coaxed.

"All right." She leaned closer, eyes flashing mischievously. "Daddy's Girls pink coconut cupcakes with raspberry filling are my all-time favorite," she whispered, and dipped her little finger into her cocktail glass. When she daintily inserted her pinkie between her lips and sucked—just for a second or two—with her eyes hot on his, Nikolas thought that the top of his head was going to blow sky-high like a ruptured steam vent.

"I usually went for the apple turnovers," he rasped. "They cost a quarter each when I was a kid."

Angelique's head tilted thoughtfully. "We used to sneak Daddy's Girls into..." she hesitated "...our boarding school and eat them after lights out. There's something so gloriously decadent about empty calories and saturated fat."

He grinned. "You're not the woman Vicki led me to expect."

Angelique looked disappointed. "I'm not?"

"Not quite."

She rolled her bottom lip between her teeth. "Then I'll have to try harder."

"Don't," he said quickly. "Don't try at all, please. Just...be."

"Just be?" she repeated, as if it was a new concept.

"Yourself," he clarified.

Angelique giggled. "Where's the fun in that?" She tossed back her head and leveled a frank look at him. "I'd rather play pretend, Niko," she purred, letting her lashes drift to half-mast.

Niko. Talk about pretend. But he liked the name coming from Angelique. It had been Vicki Neill who'd started calling him Niko, for some garbled reason he hadn't quite grasped. Usually he was called Nikolas. Nick and Nicky on occasion, but never before Niko.

Angelique touched his hand. "Tell me one thing about yourself, Niko."

"Real or pretend?"

She shrugged, again tilting her head to the side so the silken, blunt-cut ends of her hair brushed one bare shoulder. There was a small dent in her smooth, curved cheek that turned into a dimple when she smiled. He wanted her to never stop smiling.

"Whichever," she said, smiling and dimpling and

flashing her flirtatious eyes. "Then I can spend the rest of the cruise trying to discover if you've told me the truth."

He liked the sound of that. "One thing," he agreed, motioning for her to lean closer. She rested her elbows on the table and put her head near his. Her scent was light, clean, fresh—sunshine, citrus and soap.

"One thing about Nikolas Dorian," he said, pitching his voice so low she had to inch even closer, "is that he likes to kiss pretty girls named Angelique."

He caught her upper arms before she could retreat and touched his lips to her soft, open mouth. She tensed momentarily, then seemed to decide to relax and let the kiss happen. He angled his mouth over hers, feeling the warm puff of air as she released her bated breath, feeling her begin to melt as he fleetingly slid the tip of his tongue over the slickness just inside her bottom lip.

Abruptly she drew back, tilting her chin. Her eyes narrowed. "Not much mystery about the truth of that!" she said in a glittery, sophisticated voice that stole the gentle awe from what he'd thought had been a pretty darn good kiss.

Confounded, he rubbed two fingers over his newly shaved jaw.

Damn, but she was elusive!

THE CAPTAIN'S SMALL soiree was almost over when Angie and Nikolas finally showed up. Vicki, wearing a long pink dress with lime green polka dots, squealed and waved to them from across the room. "Hello, hello—over here!"

Nikolas took two champagne cocktails from a waiter and led the way to Vicki. He handed one glass to her and the other to Angie. "Sorry we're late."

Vicki tossed the end of her pink feather boa over one shoulder and posed against the grand piano with great flair. "I've been requesting show tunes, but all the pianist seems to know is classical music. Have you ever tried to sing to Bach?"

Angie laughed. "It sounds like you know how to liven up a party all on your own. You didn't need me, after all."

"In my day, I was a pistol. Now I'm only a BB gun. Funny how as soon as I turned seventy people seemed to expect me to settle down. But enough about me." Vicki eyed the pair of them. "You two seem to be getting along."

Niko traced a finger along the curve of Angie's bare shoulder. "I'm not planning on throwing this one back, Vicki. She's a keeper."

Angie resisted an impulse to rearrange the plunging neckline of her flowing white, Grecian-style gown. The thin line of heat Niko had drawn on her shoulder had oozed beneath her skin, making her breasts feel heavy and full. As her nipples peaked beneath the layers of sheer chiffon, she was shocked by her immediate desire.

Not that Niko could know that; she'd been more than obvious with him in the Voyager's Lounge. Carried away by the initial success of her masquerade—and having suddenly remembered that finger-sucking thing from a sexy movie—she'd copied the move on the spur of the moment. She'd actually felt slightly ridiculous, afraid that she'd laid it on too thick, but apparently Niko, being male, after all, hadn't thought so....

She wet her lips, thinking of his sweet kiss, and her swift misgivings that it had come about because of her lies. Being the femme fatale Angelique wasn't as uncomplicated as she'd first assumed.

"What about you, Angelique?" Vicki tilted her drink. "Do I know how to pick 'em or what?"

Angie clinked their glasses. "Yes, Vicki, you do indeed know how to pick 'em."

Vicki set her glass on the grand piano and wound her arms through the young couple's. "Let's go and introduce

Angelique to our crowd, Niko. Somehow she's managed to escape notice up to now. The Blankmores and the Cliftons were thrilled to hear there was such an adventuress on board.''

4

BY THE TIME the baked Alaska arrived at the captain's table, Angie was praying that the flaming dessert would divert attention from her. Throughout the remainder of the cocktail party and the endless courses of dinner, she'd volleyed questions like a Wimbledon champ, calling on every shred of knowledge she'd gleaned from every travel magazine and adventure story she'd ever read. When she'd gotten stuck, she'd evaded with a tinkling laugh that was intended to be charming. As a last resort, she'd lied outrageously—unless by some strange coincidence the native tribes of Borneo actually did make an aphrodisiac out of beetle dung and tree sap.

"Why, Angelique, if such an aphrodisiac truly worked, we could make a million," Vicki commented as waiters circled the table, serving the dessert. "What do you say, Virgie? Should we start a new division of the company?"

Virginia Neill rolled her eyes. "Spare me."

One of several older men at the table chuckled tolerantly. "Now, Vicki. We all know that what you gals really want is a magic love potion." He patted the jeweled hand of the silver-haired dowager beside him. "It may have been fifty years ago, but I can still remember how once we'd fallen in love my Irene had me hog-tied into marriage before I knew what hit me. Proper ladies like you all—" he beamed around the table "—want the security of love and marriage, not the physical, *ahem*, gratifications offered by an aphrodisiac."

Vicki scowled. "Says you, Bert Hassenfuss!"

He lifted a silver spoon heaped with baked Alaska to his mouth. "It's a biological fact."

Irene Hassenfuss kept still; Angie figured that at this point in the marriage an aphrodisiac held more interest for the woman, but being a "proper lady," she didn't want to shock her self-satisfied husband by admitting it.

Angie glanced at Niko to her left. Looking at him made her feel entirely improper.

"Bert's right," Virginia said. "Why deny it?"

"*You've* never married," Vicki noted. "And I've been married four times. What does that prove? Love is no guarantee."

"It does generally lead to marriage," Niko said, "which is as close to a permanent bond as our society has come."

Yet another pair of young honeymooners at the table exchanged simpering smiles and whispers. The pet name Snookums may have been involved, but Angie didn't want to listen too closely. Newlyweds were dangerous for a single girl's digestion, and she wanted to enjoy her baked Alaska as well as Niko's admiration. So long as he didn't get too carried away by agreeing with Mr. Hassenfuss, who'd looked down his nose when she'd lifted a story about her affair with a famous French artist straight out of one of Judith Krantz's novels.

"Niko, not you, too." Vicki sounded dismayed. "I thought it was just the older generation who believed women use sex to lure men into marriage."

Nikolas scrunched his brow. "Wait a minute. I didn't say—"

"Vicki!" Virginia's nostrils flared. "Really!"

"It's an interesting question," the captain said in his booming voice. The guests at his dining table all turned to listen. They could do nothing less. He cut an impressive figure with his gold-braided, white dress uniform, Teutonic good looks and authoritative, regal bearing. "If you'll permit me," he said, looking at Virginia. She gave a quick little nod, the purse of her lips betraying a hint of feminine interest even though the captain was fifteen years her junior.

"My wife is a sociologist," the captain began. A soft, cumulative sigh went up among those who'd entertained hopes. "She and I have a running debate on this subject. Which comes first—love or, as Mr. Hassenfuss put it so discreetly—physical gratification?"

Vicki leaned over the table and said in a stage whisper, "Otherwise known as *sex*." She fluttered the end of her feather boa under Niko's chin.

"Love," Virginia said firmly. "Naturally."

Several of the other women nodded in agreement.

Vicki snorted.

The captain looked up and down the table. "And as for the men?"

They glanced sidelong at each other, then down into their dessert dishes. One sought refuge in his wineglass. Another cleared his throat so many times his wife started pounding him between the shoulder blades.

"Sex."

Everyone turned to Nikolas.

"Sorry, ladies, but someone had to say it." He shrugged. "I'm afraid it *is* a biological imperative. Women want love, commitment, children. Men just want sex—at least at the beginning."

Bert Hassenfuss folded his hands over his well-padded midsection. "There you go."

His wife's face puckered.

"Are we in agreement?" queried the captain. The men nodded, avoiding the pointed stares of their wives. "And there we have the battle of the sexes, in a nutshell," the captain said. "What one side wants, the other withholds. Round and round we go."

"You might as well have asked which came first, the

chicken or the egg," Vicki said grumpily. "There is no answer."

"Depending on the relationship," one of the men qualified.

"Goodness me, yes," Vicki said brightly. "We've all had one-night stands that defy the rules."

"My word." Virginia's expression was pained. "Must you, Vicki?"

"Piffle," said her sister. "These ain't Victorian times, Virgie. Women want physical satisfaction just as much as men."

"But they still prefer to fall in love first," said a female voice from the far end of the table.

"I guarantee it," said Bert Hassenfuss at his most bombastic. "No true lady would be satisfied with the limitations of, say, a short-term shipboard fling. Even should she be persuaded to, uh, *indulge*, by the end of the cruise she would believe herself to be in love. That's the way women react." Fingering his walrus mustache, he stared frankly at Vicki, sure that he had settled the matter. "There's no logic to it—it's pure emotion."

Angie had gritted her teeth; still, a small squeak of protest leaked out.

Vicki leaned forward to see past Niko. Her smile was crafty. "Angelique, you've been so quiet. As a member of the younger generation, what do you think?"

Angie believed that both arguments had merit. But she wasn't supposed to be a levelheaded nursery school teacher from Maple Hills, Michigan, that small-town bastion of sturdy family values. She was answering in her guise as Angelique Dubonnet, and bold, daring Angelique was not the sort to deny herself any of the pleasures of life. Particularly when there was a man like Nikolas at her side, emanating enough heat to reignite the baked Alaska.

Deliberately Angie ate a spoonful of melting ice cream.

"Well, let's get one thing clear right off the bat. Just because women are emotional doesn't mean they're also illogical." Acutely aware of Niko's smoldering gaze, she licked her spoon provocatively. "That said..." she batted her lashes "...you'll have to ask the lovers I've left behind whether or not a woman is capable of a short-term affair. But, gosh, Mr. Hassenfuss, I'm afraid they just may be too lovesick to give you a coherent answer."

While Hassenfuss stammered and Vicki chortled with glee, Angie dropped her napkin on her plate and rose to her feet. Niko stared up at her, openmouthed.

He closed it with a snap when she drew her fingernail along the underside of his jaw. Teasingly she flicked his chin. "And I'll see *you* later," she purred seductively, then threw back her head and strutted out of the dining room, her skirt swishing and her hips swaying.

It was the best exit of her life.

"HERE YOU ARE," said a male voice.

Certain that Nikolas had found her, Angie whirled away from the railing, her heart leaping to her throat. "I knew—oh. It's you, Trent." She stepped back. "H-how are you doing?"

"Smooth cruisin'," he said, patting his flat stomach. "I missed you at dinner. We had two empty seats, and then the honeymooners left early, so I was stuck alone with Gina."

"Gina?"

"You know, Gina." With a leer, Trent shaped a generous hourglass in the air.

"Oh, yes." The beautician from Pittsburgh. Angie shrugged. "Sorry I skipped out on all of you, but, well, I was invited to sit at the captain's table."

Trent whistled. "How'd you manage that?"

Angie fluttered her fingers noncommittally. "Connections, I suppose."

He narrowed his eyes. "Can you hook me up?"

"Well, I…"

While she fumbled for excuses, he was looking her over. "Whoa, Angie, babe, you sure know how to fix yourself up. I hardly recognize you."

"It's just a haircut," she said. *And a new attitude.*

Trent sidled closer, hands in his pockets, slouched like an imitation James Dean. "How about me and you heading down to my cabin for some one-on-one—"

A woman's voice trilled from one of the brightly lit stairwells. "Trent? You up here, honey?"

Angie took another step back. A bigger one this time. "Sounds like someone's looking for you."

"That's just Gina," he said, with a dismissive shrug as he lit a cigarette. "I can lose her if you're interested.…" He shifted his shoulders as if the sight of his chest rippling beneath a tight black, raw silk T-shirt would make Angie swoon.

"No," she said firmly. "Thank you just the same."

Gina poked her head out on deck and called, "Honey, I thought you were going to help me spend my money in the casino?"

Trent took a deep drag and flicked the cigarette into the water. Angie pressed herself against the railing as he deliberately brushed against her on his way to the stairs. Plumes of smoke poured from his nostrils. "If you change your mind…"

"I don't see that happening."

"Your loss, babe."

Angie watched him go, relieved that he had, but alarmed by the thought that her blatant flirtations might have seemed just as sleazy to Nikolas. Had she gone too far, too fast? Could she possibly blame her extraordinary physical appetite for him on too much sea air, too much exposure to sappy-sweet newlyweds, too much of the valentine-themed giddiness?

And three champagne cocktails, she added. There had to be some tangible reason for her actions.

Some reason other than sheer love-at-first-holiday-sighting.

Did it matter why? What was done was done, but at least they hadn't done *it* yet. Even though she'd raced back to her cabin after dinner, panicked at the thought of going through with it, but still having the wherewithal to know she should be armed with a condom, just in case....

Angie clutched her purse and looked up and down the promenade for signs of Niko. The evening was balmy; many couples were out strolling the deck, gazing at the stars, holding hands, smooching. Circling the entire deck might take a good ten minutes, but she'd been sure that Niko would find her here.

After Angelique had more or less promised herself to him, how could he resist?

She started walking, feeling too conspicuous in her solitude to stand around mooning at the ocean. Particularly when everybody else seemed to have paired up, from senior citizens to Trent and Gina. This wasn't the way she'd imagined spending her *second* night at sea, either.

"Angelique," Nikolas said from one of the long, low deck chairs beneath the overhang.

Angie stopped. She'd been so self-absorbed she'd almost walked past him.

"I was wondering if you'd let that guy pick you up," he said.

So he'd been watching her the entire time! What did *that* mean? She collapsed onto the chair beside him, her hands clenched on her purse with the condom in it. "Oh, that was—that was just some guy who..." Remembering to be Angelique, she summoned forth the airy laugh. "You know what they say. Many try, but few succeed."

"Something like climbing Mount Everest?"

Angie squared her shoulders. "The summit *is* breathtaking."

"Oh, I've no doubt of that."

She shivered. Niko's voice was the sexiest thing she'd ever heard.

"Would you like my jacket?" he asked, and slipped his white dinner jacket around her shoulders before she could answer. When he kept his arm around her, hugging her warmly, she decided that words weren't necessary, and laid her head against his chest with a soft sigh. *This* was how she'd imagined her second night at sea.

Most men would have brought up the dinner conversation without delay. Not Niko.

Finding it easier and easier to abandon her previous inhibitions, Angie snuggled closer. Soon she was halfway onto his chair. His arm slipped a little lower, his fingers brushing a lazy caress over her bare arm beneath the jacket. She murmured approval, her skin prickled by needle points of desire.

She tangled one leg with Niko's, finding something provocative in the contrast of her exposed limb and strappy gold sandal against his black trousers and shiny patent leather loafers. He murmured his own approval, making each one of her plum-colored toenails tingle.

Her hand slid along his shirtfront. "There are wild rumors about you floating around this ship, you know, Nikolas Dorian." She moved her cheek so she could see his face. "Some say you're an arms dealer, here to scope out your smuggling operation. Others say you're an undercover cop trying to *catch* an arms dealer. If that's the case, I'd check out Bert Hassenfuss."

Niko smiled. "I'll keep that in mind."

"You're also a real estate swindler, an architect from Yale and a Greek millionaire-fisherman's son. You may even be Salman Rushdie with a total body makeover, but I'm not putting much credence in that one."

His smiled broadened. "And I'm not telling."

Angie tugged on his black bow tie. "Aw, c'mon, Niko. Who are you?"

He put his right hand on her waist and pulled her closer, sliding her body up along his—a few millimeters of tantalizing friction. "I'm just a guy who likes to kiss girls named Angelique."

5

NIKO'S BREATH WAS WARM on her face as his lips grazed her cheek, her jaw, her chin. The flurry of her heartbeat filled her ears.

Soothing her with sweet nothings, he petted the curve of her hip. He put his face into her hair and breathed deeply. He nuzzled her ear, his lips warm and gentle as they found their way along her neck to the hollow of her throat. She clutched at his shoulders, astonished at just how desperate she was for more. And in response he went even slower, drawing out each of the voluptuous pleasures he took in her body until she wanted to scream.

Although she succeeded in holding her tongue, she was also trembling all over with anticipation by the time Niko's lips finally reached hers. Sighing in sweet relief, she went lax against the length of him, the riveting contact of their mouths all that she needed to quench her aching desires.

Niko played with her mouth, gently and generously. Coaxing every last flavor and sensation out of each kiss, he slid his tongue against hers, his lips nibbling and plucking and suckling.

She was half on top of him by then, her legs intertwined with his. The rest of the world—and its rules—had dropped away. Her overnight makeover into a playful, promiscuous party girl was complete. Why else would she have dared to take his hand and put it inside her gaping neckline?

He palmed the weight of her breast, eagerly scraping

away the cup of her satin bra to release her puckered nipple. "*Niko,*" she said, squirming against him. Even through the layers of their clothing, his arousal felt hot and hard, blatantly demanding pressed against her thighs. The answering demand grew inside her, down low, down deep.

She levered herself up, lifting her torso just enough so that he had access to the bare breast pressed into the V of her dress. He moaned and grasped the edges of the jacket still draped around her shoulders, using it to shield their actions from passersby. With his lips he delicately took the peak into the heat of his mouth. She shuddered. Desire pulsed through her veins so strongly that she was propelled to press more of her breast into his mouth, her fingers threaded through his thick black hair. Niko opened wider, eating at her flesh, sucking her nipple into the hot depths until she was slick with desire, incoherent in her flooding need.

This was not at all like Angie Dubonnet. And, oh, my, was she ever glad of that!

Niko's hips thrust against hers. "Yes," she said, her hand flying like an arrow to the heart of his response.

He caught her wrist in the nick of time. "No."

She froze. "No?"

"Not here," he said, panting. "Not now."

Somewhere in the recesses of her previous mind-set, she knew he was right; she couldn't get her newly impassioned body to agree, though. "My cabin...?" she suggested in a small, breathless voice, forgetting that her cabin wasn't up to his standards.

Niko's face was drawn into harsh lines. The tendons of his neck had gone rigid and his eyes glittered with passion. Or pain. "Not tonight," he said, and groaned when her thigh brushed against his erection.

He doesn't want me, she thought in silent fear. But almost instantly she knew that she was wrong. Niko wanted her;

how much he wanted her was stamped on his face, on his body. On hers.

He wanted her, but he was being prudent, much as she'd once been. Ruefully she slid off his lap, pulling the jacket closer, fumbling beneath it to adjust her clothing over the shocking evidence of her dampened breast.

She flipped her hair off her face. "Why not tonight?" The lilt of insouciance she'd tried for didn't quite come off. Her makeover wasn't as complete as all that.

"There are some things we should consider first."

Angie glanced over the promenade. "Like location?" she suggested. Most of the passengers had gone on to other amusements for the evening, but there were still several people out and about, enjoying the star-sprinkled evening. Farther along the deck another couple leaned against the railing, glued together, kissing passionately.

"Not exactly." Niko took a ragged breath. "I was thinking about what we discussed at dinner."

"Oh, that."

"Yes, that."

Angie felt herself blushing. She fixed her gaze on the moon, hung low over the water, three-quarters full. It painted a silver streak on the midnight blue ocean.

"I was merely being...provocative," she whispered. She cleared her throat, trying to smile. "Entertaining the old folks."

"Then you didn't mean what you said—about being capable of a short-term sexual relationship?"

His tone confused her. "Oh, so you want me to admit that women are at the mercy of their emotions, unable to participate in a shipboard fling without turning it into a *love* affair?"

Nikolas leaned forward, putting his feet to the deck, his legs spread on either side of the chaise. "I'm not suggesting there's anything wrong in short-term affairs. It's just the way things usually work out."

Angie closed her eyes. To be honest, it was becoming apparent to her that what she wanted even more than to make love to Niko for the rest of the cruise was to make love to Niko for the rest of her life. She knew her response was instinctual, impulsive, *highly* emotional, but at least it was honest. Heartbreakingly honest.

Angelique, however...Angelique was another kettle of fish. What in the world would a woman like Angelique want?

Angie opened her eyes, concentrating on the moon again as she slipped out of the white dinner jacket and negligently tossed it at Nikolas. "I'm not like most women."

He caught the jacket. "That's obvious."

She got up and walked over to the railing. "I want the sun and the moon and everything in between," she said fervently, then turned to face Nikolas with her arms stretched against the rail. Her white chiffon dress fluttered in the breeze, the slit flapping open to reveal her legs. Striving to appear unconcerned, she crossed one ankle over the other, her silk hose shimmering in the moonlight. "But I can get all of that for myself. What I want from you is simple—five days and nights of hot, fabulous sex. When we dock in Miami, we say goodbye. No strings attached."

Triumphantly she threw back her head, watching Niko's changing expression through narrowed eyes. Her heart was thumping like crazy; adrenaline shot through her veins. And still she managed to stay still and poised, as cool as though she spoke so boldly as a matter of course. If Niko was the playboy he appeared to be, and Angelique was anything close to the femme fatale she was pretending to be, his response to her offer would be automatic.

Why, then, was he hesitating?

THE NEXT MORNING, the *Sea Siren* was anchored off a tiny, picture-postcard island called—rather unimaginatively—Paradise. Most of the passengers took the tender that ran between the ship and the harbor, disgorging them into the small marketplace and six miles of pristine white sand beaches. Angie was ready to sign up for the first trip until Nikolas informed her that he'd made plans. He had chartered a private motorboat that would take them somewhere better than Paradise.

Their destination turned out to be a deserted island too tiny to have a name. There was no marketplace, no harbor, no other people in sight, only emerald forest, white sand and blue water.

"I sure hope your 'chauffeur' understood when to retrieve us." She moved through the clear turquoise water toward a crescent of sandy beach. "Beautiful as this place is, I don't relish the thought of being stranded here after dark."

Niko, a picnic basket on one shoulder and an awkward, lumpy bundle on the other, cocked an eyebrow at her, his teeth flashing in the sunshine when he smiled. "Hmm, I don't know. I like the idea of playing Robinson Crusoe. Think of it—just you and me and the endless deep blue sea."

"And the sharks, and the jellyfish, and the thriving insect population," she said in a cheerful singsong.

While Nikolas was busy setting up his beach-party gear, she opened her bag, pulled out the batik scarf she'd bought in Nassau and tied it around her hips, sarong-style.

Much better, she thought, toeing off her sopping beach shoes. No matter how many hours she put in on the treadmill and the step machine, she was always going to carry an extra few inches around her hips. She'd accepted the womanly nature of her figure; she'd learned to appreciate her body's strength and health and productivity. But just the same…

It would be okay if they were both naked. Which, perversely enough, seemed to work both ways—how could she worry about the size of her behind when there was a naked man in front of her?

Particularly if the naked man was Niko.

She stared unseeingly at the ocean, her cheeks warming. Would the naked man *ever* be Niko?

"Angie?" he said, breaking through her daze. "Angie, we've only been here five minutes. You can't be suffering from sunstroke that quickly."

"I'm fine." She put on her sunglasses. "Just fine."

"You aren't still mad about last night?"

She swallowed nervously. After their showdown on the promenade deck, Nikolas had begun silently walking her back to her cabin, with the terms of their relationship still up in the air. She'd started panicking inside, both at her audacious actions and at the looming prospect of inviting him into her decidedly unheiresslike cabin on the C deck. So she'd silkily pressed up against him in the upper-deck corridor and let him think it had been his idea to kiss her until her hair curled. Then she'd made some excuse or other about the night being young and the casino calling her name. She'd left him there and raced down to her cabin, where she'd spent the rest of the night tossing and turning. Her body had been and still was all revved up like a dragster that hadn't made it off the starting line.

"Of course I'm not mad. Why would I be mad because you've got some sort of complex about shipboard flings?" She snapped a towel across the sand. "Why would that make me mad?"

Disappointed and frustrated, sure, but not mad, she added silently. She was too itchy with longings to hold on to an emotion as unrewarding as anger.

"I figured we ought to take this a bit more slowly,"

Nikolas said, peeling off his tank top. The water droplets caught in the curly triangle of his chest hair glistened in the sunlight.

Wobbly as a toddler, Angie dropped to her knees on the towel. She summoned up flirtatious laugher. "Right, Niko. Good call. A deserted island's the perfect spot for restraint."

Judging by the level of his lowering eyelids, he was staring at her breasts, thinly covered by a damp orange tank swimsuit. Her nipples grew traitorously tight under the heat of his gaze. "Maybe you should have invited Virginia Neill along as chaperon," she said.

"I'm not that noble."

"And I'm not noble at all." Angie pulled various items out of her beach bag until she found the baggy T-shirt that had been folded and tucked away at the bottom.

When she started to put it on, Nikolas stopped her with his hand on her wrist. "You won't need a cover-up."

She could think of only one reason why not.

"See?" He pointed at the asymmetrical shade tent he'd just set up. It was made of white canvas, stretched taut on poles plunged into the sand. "I didn't want you to get sunburned."

"Oh," Angie said stupidly. And here she'd hoped that he wanted her uncovered for his own private delectation.

"That, too," he said.

She flinched as his hand curved around her waist. "Wha-what?"

"I want you, Angie." The pressure of his palm brought her hips flush against his. "I want you naked in the surf, naked in the sand, naked in the sun."

All the air whooshed out of her lungs.

He whispered directly into her ear. "I want you naked in my arms."

"What happened to taking our time?" she asked, panting against the smooth velvety skin of his shoulders. She breathed in the scent of primal male. Heat and lust thickened her blood, slowing her actions and reactions to the level of a sensuous dream. Much like the one she'd had last night.

Niko nibbled on her bottom lip for a precious few seconds before he released her. He grinned at her obvious confusion. "I was just letting you know that I don't have any complexes regarding shipboard flings," he explained.

"*Ohh.*"

"But neither do I perform on command," he added.

She took that optimistically. There was hope for them yet. Slowly she removed her sunglasses, letting him see the truth of her feelings for him in her wide eyes. "I'm fine with that," she said, still a trifle breathless. "So why don't you—" she shrugged, her body already aching with anticipation "—umm, surprise me?"

He smiled. "I can do that."

Somehow she managed to get to her feet. She stumbled in the sand, then found her legs and ran toward the lagoon, untying her sarong as she went. "Race you to the water!" she yelled over her shoulder, releasing the red print scarf on a gust of wind.

THE ISLAND HEAT lay heavy on Nikolas's skin. He could barely lift his eyelids; raising his head off the sand was out of the question.

Angelique lay on her back beside him, breathing deeply in sleep. Her pale skin had taken on a rosy, golden tone in the past few days. Tiny freckles had sprung up on her nose and the sweet pink curves of her cheeks. When she licked her lips, he held his breath, waiting, but she only smiled to herself, languidly shimmying her shoulders to find a comfortable position before drifting off again.

He moved his hand an inch so he could touch the

strands of hair fanned across her rumpled towel, and even that was enough to make his heart contract.

Nikolas let out a weighty sigh. What was he going to do about Angie?

6

AFTER SWIMMING and sunning, after they'd plowed through the picnic lunch provided by the cruise ship, she'd asked why he'd taken to calling her Angie. He couldn't explain, other than to say that she just seemed like an Angie to him. She'd wrinkled her nose. But there'd been a hint of satisfaction there, too, and he wondered why.

Just another of her mysteries, he decided.

What *was* he going to do about Angie?

He wasn't the man she thought he was, but then she wasn't the woman she wanted him to think she was, either. He knew that much; he just hadn't been able to figure out whether or not that meant her offer of a shipboard fling was legitimate. It was killing him to delay—witness the hard-on carving a depression into the sand packed beneath him. And just because he'd touched her damn hair.

They'd hung mosquito netting in swoops and swags from pole to pole, turning the canvas tent into a sort of gauzy, exotic love grotto. Thick heat oozed through the gaps, rising off the blinding white sand outside their tent like steam in a sauna. Angie had been dozing for twenty minutes now, and Nikolas very much wanted her to wake up, even though straining his brain had drenched him in sweat. More strenuous activities could cause serious damage.

He rocked slightly on his stomach and groaned, certain that he'd *already* suffered permanent damage.

The glaring sunshine bounced off the white canvas

shade and filtered through the netting, dappling their shadowy refuge with a lustrous, buttery light. Angie sleeping was a beautiful sight. Her skin was misted with a fine sheen of perspiration, her chest rising and falling with each breath, the zipper on the front of her swimsuit open just far enough to bare the tempting swells of her breasts.

Nikolas found that he could move, after all. He hooked one finger in the metal ring attached to her zipper and eased it down as far as her ribs. She stirred, but didn't waken. He supposed that what he was doing was wrong, even though she *had* asked him to surprise her. In his need he forgot his worry over unanswered questions about the basis of their relationship. All he knew was that he couldn't wait for her any longer.

He peeled back one side of the stretchy fabric, revealing her breast: smooth, creamy, luscious. Fine grains of sand clung here and there. He touched her softened nipple with one fingertip to flick off the sand and wound up circling the areola with feather-fine strokes until her response became physical.

Angelique's lashes fluttered. Nikolas lifted his head and shoulders off the sand, edging closer so his face would fill her field of vision. A small smile flitted across her lips.

"Surprise," he said, and put his mouth over her breast.

She gasped and arched off the towel. "Nikolas!" He fluttered his tongue against her nipple, and her voice melted into a slumberous purr that dripped over him like warm syrup. "Oh, Niko…"

Closing her eyes, she let her head loll as he framed her breast with his hands and laved it extravagantly. He glanced up at her face. She seemed vulnerable in her newly wakened state, fragile and precious, so he touched her more gently, slowing his passion to a stream of wet, plucking, openmouthed kisses.

"What a delicious way to wake up," she said softly. "May I take you home as my alarm clock?"

"If I'll fit into your luggage."

His tongue swirled over her pebbled nipple; she breathed a long sigh of contentment. "Oh, I'll pay the extra freight, don't worry about that."

"Then take me home, baby," he said, licking kisses across her chest to the base of her throat. He felt her swallow, hard.

The rhythmic swoosh of the waves filled the silence. They lay together, breathing heavily in the heat—damp, warm, skin on skin. Angie put her arms around him and said, "Make love to me, Niko." Just that, no more.

Exactly, he thought, less pleased than sad, if only Angie knew it.

But he held her face in his hands and kissed her, tasting salt and sea and the sweet tropical fruits they'd eaten for dessert. "You taste like paradise," he murmured, dipping between her parted lips in search of her tongue. She curled it against his teeth, mimicking the waves of melting warmth that curled through his swelling body. He pulsed with heat, with hunger.

Angie wrapped herself around him, her slick skin slithering against his. They kissed and caressed and then, finally, he sat back to roll her swimsuit past her hips. His fingers felt thick and slow, brushing over her legs and the soft skin of her thighs to the point where her deep, wet heat blossomed into succulence.

She inhaled sharply between her teeth when he touched her, but lifted her body into his intimate caress like a moth seeking the oblivion of a flame. A late afternoon breeze rolled in off the ocean, billowing the scrim of mosquito netting. Its cool embrace did nothing to abate their urgency.

"Come inside me now," Angie said, reaching for Niko through the miasma that had blurred her emotional responses into something that felt a lot like love. Because she'd responded before fully waking, she hadn't been able to calculate her reactions. Which meant there was no playacting, but no inhibitions, either.

Niko's body was hard against hers, seething with such hot passion that she shuddered at the thought of having him inside her. Was she still dreaming, or had their feelings for each other become tangible, as alive as the sun and the silken sand and the needs so commanding they were clumsy and breathless in their haste to meet them? Panting, Niko kicked away his trunks and rolled on top of her, pressing his weight upon her, stealing her breath again as he slowly slid deeper and deeper inside her till there was no place left to go. Together they were complete, and the sensation was such that Angie forgot everything but her need for Niko—Niko's body, Niko's love.

They were graceful now, melded into a glorious one. And they were part of the heat, *inside* the heat, suffused by it, breathing it deep into their parched lungs. "Come now," Angie whispered, flooding with her own fertile climax. Niko's breath sounded harsh in the quiet tent as he pumped inside her, turning their mutual effluence into the liquid fire of fusion.

THE REMAINDER OF the cruise spun like a kaleidoscope—a shifting, changing mélange of colorful memories filled with laughter and sun and starry black velvet nights. Angie wanted to experience everything, and she brought Nikolas along for the ride as the *Sea Siren* stopped in San Juan, Puerto Rico and Saint Thomas. They shopped, swam, sunned, danced. They played tourist, taking a hundred photographs. On board, they participated in every activity they could find time for, including making valentines with the activities director and a dozen gray-haired ladies, and taking part in an A deck splash party that culminated in a sweethearts-only blindfold bareback water polo match.

By the next-to-last day of the cruise, Angie was sun-burned, overfed and nearly played out. She'd pretty much dropped her Angelique Dubonnet act—except when Vicki or one of her circle asked for another of Angelique's outrageous stories. Then, depending on the level of her energy or daiquiri consumption, Angie would wax ridiculous with tales of skiing Zermatt with Alberto Tomba and trekking the Australian outback with a blue-eyed jackaroo and six angry camels who'd rather spit in your eye than follow orders. If Niko commented, it was usually to ask with a smile if she'd tried on Tomba's gold medals and spat back at the jackaroo. She felt, sometimes, that he was toying with her. Which was sort of okay, because it was no less than she toyed with him....

By mutual silent consent they did not speak of what they did to each other, and for each other, and *with* each other every night. And, actually, every day. All their explanations, reassurances and promises were delivered in the silent language of lovers—the touch of their clasped hands, the soft gasp in the night, the poignancy of their kisses as the ship swung around and sailed for its home port.

On Friday afternoon, Valentine's Day, which was their last full day on ship, Angie returned to the small cabin she'd been using as no more than a pit stop. The steward had straightened up again, after she'd dashed in that morning to look for her last pair of clean underwear and a dry bathing suit.

She found two envelopes on the small fold-down table by the bed. The first was a fancy, deckle-edged invitation to the gala Valentine Ball that evening, something of a misnomer since every passenger was invited for the price of the cruise. Angie had been saving her nicest dress for the occasion, but she wondered if there was still time to make an appointment at the shipboard salon. Her new hairdo hadn't stood up to the activities of the past week—it was now more of a haystack than a chic bob.

She sat on the bed and opened the second envelope. Inside was a valentine from Nikolas—handmade in the arts-and-crafts class that had been one of their shipboard activities. Aside from a bewildered gentleman in a wheelchair, Niko had been the only male in the cut-and-paste group. All the older ladies had fussed over him; he'd enlisted their aid in keeping his work of art out of Angie's radar range.

The valentine made her want to cry. It wasn't very creative, or even very neat, but that didn't matter. She was a sucker for sentiment. Back home, her walls, closets and scrapbooks were jammed with handmade tokens from the children she worked with. Niko's paper-doily, red-construction-paper heart was a cut above the crayon scrawls she received from the children, but the emotion of it was just as heartfelt. "Roses are red," he'd written, "my feelings true blue/This day is complete/if I share it with you." Below that, in a bold masculine hand, it was signed: "Love, Nikolas."

Love? A tear slipped from the corner of Angie's eye. Was there a chance that Nikolas actually loved her?

All along she'd been telling herself that she could handle the emotional ramifications of a shipboard romance that was sure to end when the *Sea Siren* berthed in Miami. If the woman Niko had been involved with wasn't quite Angelique, she wasn't quite Angie, either. The perplexity of that had caused her some misgivings, but she'd made herself cherish every moment of her time with Niko instead of dwelling on regrets about what might have been. Reality would intervene soon enough, and she sincerely doubted that the romance would survive.

She'd thought she was prepared for that.

Oh, but this valentine—!

"I GOT EIGHT VALENTINES," Vicki boasted, "and only three of them were from women friends."

"You've been a busy girl," Angie said, looking out over the glamorous, glittering crowd. The ballroom was decorated with silver balloons, red crepe paper, lacy hearts and twinkling fairy lights. A ten-piece orchestra was taking requests for love songs. "It sounds like you've become the belle of the ship."

Vicki waggled a gloved finger beneath Angie's nose. "Not so fast, my dear. I do believe that title goes to you." The diamond tennis bracelet Vicki wore over her elbow-length white gloves matched the tiara perched atop her strawberry blond pouf. "All the passengers are talking about Niko, the Greek millionaire, and his inamorata, Angelique the adventuress."

Angie gazed fondly at Vicki. "If that's true, it's only because you're always urging them on." Tonight she didn't care to worry about her charade and its impending conclusion, so a change of subject was in order. "Tell me about those valentines, Vicki. I thought you were complaining that the supply of available men was rather limited."

Vicki giggled. "Not when you count the crew."

"Oh, my."

"And married men, too. Not that I encourage that sort of attention. Would you believe that Bert Hassenfuss made a pass at me?"

Angie's eyes widened. "And I would have picked him as a good candidate for Viagra."

Vicki fluffed the red rose corsage pinned to her shoulder. "I didn't say he *succeeded*." She scanned the crowd. "Look, there's one of my sweethearts, dancing without his cane. And here comes Niko—he finally got away from Irene Hassenfuss. I believe I'll leave you two lovebirds alone." Vicki picked up her skirt and made her way toward the dance floor, executing a pirouette in her three-inch heels. "Oh, to be fifty again!" she called over her shoulder, making Angie laugh.

Nikolas arrived at her side. "Talking to Vicki again, I see," he observed as the orchestra launched into "The Blue Danube."

"She reminds me of my grandmother. They're both spunky and full of life."

Niko cocked an eyebrow. "I didn't think Angelique Dubonnet admitted to relatives as regular as grandmothers. A diamond-laden matriarch, perhaps, ensconced somewhere in a ritzy family mansion?"

Was he fishing? Angie didn't know how to respond. She no longer particularly cared to continue her charade; her feelings for Nikolas had gone deeper than that. "Oh, you," she resorted to saying, batting at his arm. "Well, since we're here and all dolled up, let's dance, shall we? Do you know how to waltz?"

Niko took her into his arms. "I can fake it."

Me, too, she thought as they swept onto the dance floor. Unfortunately, she'd managed to fake it just a little too well. Or, looking at it from the point of view of her soon-to-be-broken heart, not nearly well enough.

She'd expected Angelique Dubonnet to break hearts. Just not her own.

7

"DID I REMEMBER to tell you how handsome you are in a tuxedo?" Angie asked Niko once they'd left the Valentine Ball, having had their fill of dance, drink and the midnight buffet.

"Once or twice."

"You'll look even better out of it," she whispered as they stepped off the elevator. It was an oft-used line, but so true. For some reason, Niko had asked to go to her cabin tonight, just as he'd asked to dine at her assigned table the previous evening. She'd finally decided to explain away the lack of first class amenities with a story about booking her ticket at the last minute when little choice of accommodations had remained. But as she nervously ran away at the mouth, explaining far more than necessary, she began to get the feeling that Niko knew the excuse was an excuse.

Angie was jolted into silence. And what if he knew even more than that? But he couldn't. *He's still with me, right?*

In the corridor, they happened upon Trent and Gina, who were about to let themselves into a nearby cabin. Trent had the grace to look sheepish. Gina was triumphant in red satin. "Guess what?" she said, holding up a bulging evening bag. "I hit the jackpot playing the slots! Won me two thousand bucks, enough to pay Trent's airfare to Pittsburgh—and then some!"

Angie was genuinely glad that her tablemates had also had a good cruise. "Congratulations," Niko said, having met the other pair when he'd taken the empty chair at their table. "I think," he added after ushering Angie inside and closing the cabin door.

"Oh, Trent's not such a bad sort," she said, more generous now that she was safely removed from his advances. Of course, Angelique might not be so kind. "Sleazy, certainly," she scornfully added, then couldn't help amending that, too. "I guess he just tries too hard."

Niko put his arms around her waist. "He tried for you, I know. Good thing he's not your type."

She cocked her head. "Yes, I already had my eye on Niko Dorian, the Greek millionaire."

A shadow crossed his face. "That's Vicki's story."

"It's not true, then?"

"Only partly."

Angie didn't want to know which part was true, not tonight. And maybe never. She tried to think of tomorrow, the first day of the rest of her life without Nikolas, but the thought was so upsetting she had to rest her head against his chest and fight back tears. Angelique would be living for the moment, she reminded herself, particularly when they had only one more precious night together. Despite her conflicted emotions, could she manage to be Angelique for just a little while longer?

"Hold me," she said to Nikolas, pressing her fists against his lapels. She nudged her way past his starched collar, her lips seeking the cleft in his chin, the pleasure of his warm lips. "Kiss me, Niko. Please."

"No problem." His voice was...strained. "I do like to kiss pretty girls."

"Named Angelique," she said with a sigh, but that didn't bother her as much as it might have. Angelique was just a lot of fancy trimmings; Nikolas had been making love to *Angie.* Which was some comfort for her to take back home.

"Angie," he whispered, sinking his fingers into her hair

so he could tilt back her head and kiss her most thoroughly. Angie enjoyed herself—most thoroughly. After a while his hands slid to her derriere to tug her firmly up against himself, and she liked that just as much, surrendering with a willing sigh to the plunder of his mouth. She simmered with fresh desire; around Niko, desire was an infinitely renewable resource.

He left her to click on the radio. "My Funny Valentine" was playing. "Should we order champagne," he asked, slaking his thirst at her mouth, "or strawberries—" nibbling her earlobe "—or perhaps a squeeze bottle of honey?" His tongue licked a ticklish path along the upper slopes of her breasts.

Laughing, she tightened her arms around his shoulders. "There's more than enough here to satisfy all my appetites." Thank heaven he could always make her laugh, even when she knew that this was their last time together. And so, most likely, did he. The only difference was that afterward he would probably go on without looking back, just as Angelique was supposed to.

His hands went again to her bottom, wordlessly encouraging her to sway to the soft music. "Have I told you how beautiful you are tonight?"

"Once or twice." A hundred times might last her through the rest of the winter.

"Is that all?" he said. "How neglectful." His breath ruffled her upswept locks. "Your hair is beautiful." He kissed the hollow of her throat beneath the small winking diamond of her best necklace; with his fingertips he flicked her gold hoop earrings. "And this, and these."

He ran his hands over her floor-length black velvet gown. Angie was immersed in bliss even before he murmured, "Beautiful..." When he touched her face with reverence, she nearly swooned. "So very beautiful."

Her eyes filled. "Nikolas..." She hesitated. "I have to tell you—"

He stopped her with a kiss. "Shh. Not tonight."

She nodded in understanding. *This is the nature of ship-board romances*, she told herself. By next week, they'd be only fond memories to each other.

Nikolas slipped the strap of her dress off one shoulder and she responded with a shivering arousal despite her sadness. Okay, then, they'd be *spicy* memories to each other, especially after he got a look at the incredible lingerie she'd found in one of the ship's boutiques. It wasn't Angie's style at all, but Angelique, of course, was another matter....

And I am Angelique, for one last night. I can be reckless and daring and intensely sexual. Niko used his teeth to pull down her other strap, and Angie had to lock her knees to keep from falling. She closed her eyes. *Or at least I can do my best to fake it.*

With a deep sigh, she gave herself—and Angelique—up to the tumult of physical desires flooding her body. Drowning was supposed to be the easiest way to go....

"Black Velvet" by Alannah Myles came on the radio, perhaps the sexiest, most sultry song ever recorded. It seemed a strange coincidence, because Nikolas had already unzipped Angie's fitted black velvet gown and was kneeling before her, peeling it away in the faint silvery glow of the star-filled porthole. "Black velvet," he said, his arms filling with the stuff as she stepped out of the dress.

"If you please," she purred, lifting one lissome leg to place her high-heeled shoe on his shoulder. She was clad in a black Victorian corset that made her breasts jut erotically, a teeny-tiny pair of black silk panties and opaque black stockings. Plus the shoes, one of whose lethal heels was biting into his shoulder.

There was a manic edge to Angie tonight. She'd been so apologetic about her modest cabin, even though he hadn't bothered to pretend to care. And once they were inside, she'd bounced from sad to sexy in the snap of his fingers, gone in a flash from teariness to eyes glittering with decadent promise. As he had several times in the past few days, he sensed the struggle within her, the close-your-eyes-and-swallow-hard acceptance of their short-term affair. He'd begun to doubt that she was ever going to admit to the truth about herself. And about their feelings for each other.

For now, though—for tonight—was he a bastard for using her present erotically charged mood to his advantage?

Not when he knew what he knew, Nikolas decided. Tomorrow would be soon enough for Angie to learn *his* truth, whether or not she revealed her own, and then he'd see to it that she never stopped smiling again.

In the meantime, he was kneeling before her, the scent of her feminine arousal enough to turn the best of a man's intentions to lust. Taking her foot in his hand, he slipped off the shoe, kissed her sole and suddenly gave her leg a quick, hard jerk. She let out a cry and toppled over onto the bed. Before she could recover, he was on her, parting her thighs to make his place.

Laughing, Angie beat at his chest with the flats of her hands. He captured her wrists and pressed them to the bed, looming over her with his lips curving into a wicked, lopsided smile. The tussle had made her breasts pop entirely out of the corset, and he couldn't resist leaning down to take one rosy crest into his mouth. He milked it, flicking his tongue against the stiff nipple. It wasn't long before she relaxed into a contented sprawl, her eyelids closing as she purred beneath her breath. "Mmm, that's lovely, Niko."

He pinched the other nipple.

Her eyes flew open.

Wanting to have her naked, he ran his fingers over the tight corset, trying to figure out how to get the contraption off her. "Get rid of this thing," he said, finally giving up on the row of tiny hooks and eyes.

She pushed at him. "Get off me then, you brute. And see to your own clothing while you're at it."

He rose and slowly removed his tuxedo, piece by piece. Angie had made quick work of her undergarments—she left the stockings on—and then made herself at home, tucked cozily into the narrow bed, watching him with her eyes slitted like a cat's. "There's not room for two in this bed," she said when he was finished and standing before her in his birthday suit. Pouting, she studied him through her lashes. "It's a shame."

Nikolas felt himself stiffening even though he'd thought it was impossible to be any more aroused. "I can think of a way."

She grinned, beckoning with a curled finger. "There's something to be said for not thinking." She opened the blanket and slid farther down the bed, presenting herself to him. "C'mere."

Recklessly aroused, he mounted her. She wrapped her silk-clad legs around his waist, clinging like a limpet as he reached down to find her wet, silken warmth. "I *know* I can fit," he said between clenched teeth, stroking deeper to prepare her.

Angie grasped his erection and arched upward with her hips; obviously she didn't want to wait. Nikolas let her guide the way, clamping his jaw to hold back his primal urges until the penetration was complete. She curved into him, rocking her hips in a rhythm that had become as familiar as the motion of the ship cutting through the waves.

"Nikolas!" she said, gasping. He took her mouth, kissing her deeply, sucking on her tongue as she pressed her palms to his spine, holding him as if otherwise he would leave. "Make me not think," she pleaded, and all he could do was shelter her body beneath his as their passion crested and the waves of oblivion crashed over them.

8

THE MORNING FLEW BY, and Angie was glad of it in a grim sort of way. She was just as glad that she was leaving for the airport directly from the dock. She couldn't see prolonging the agony.

She packed quickly, trying not to think about how each piece of clothing represented a time with Niko. The white Grecian dress with the daring slit. The blue-and-gold *Sea Siren* T-shirt he'd bought for her in the gift shop after he'd tossed her in the pool on a dare and soaked what she was wearing. The short skirt she'd worn in Saint Thomas, the one Niko had slid his hand up when they were supposed to be listening to an earnest young tour guide.

At that, Angie slammed shut her suitcase and ran to find Vicki, who would cheer her up as surely as the sun would set on her first day without Niko.

Angie was calm by the time they began to disembark. Nikolas was with her, holding her hand. She knew she was being a child, waiting until the very last minute to make her confession, but she just hadn't been able to bring herself to do it earlier. As they made their way down the gangplank, she decided that now was the time.

Tilting up the brim of her straw hat, she turned to look back at the ship. It loomed against the sky, gleaming white in the sunshine. "Goodbye," she whispered. "Goodbye, Angelique."

Niko inclined his head. "Hmm?"

Angie glanced past him. A line of taxicabs waited near the dock. After she motioned to one of the drivers and he began loading her luggage, she knew she couldn't put it off any longer.

"Nikolas, there's something I have to tell you. Maybe you've already guessed." He started to speak and she put her hand to his mouth, touching his lips with her fingertips. "No, don't say anything yet. The only way I can get through this is if I do it all at once, fast, like pulling off a bandage."

"All right," he said equably, twining his fingers through hers once again. He gave her hand a little squeeze of encouragement.

He knew. Angie couldn't smile, even though she now saw how absurd it was for her to masquerade as a jet-setting adventuress. Probably everyone on board had been laughing behind her back at her far-fetched stories.

She studied Niko, so handsome and clean and sexy in a pale blue shirt and jeans. The sea breeze had feathered his thick hair across his forehead, and his eyes were dark and kind, watching her with a tender patience that was more than she deserved. She thrust her hand into her unclasped straw bag, seeking comfort in Niko's valentine. She didn't withdraw it, just held it in her hand with her other arm clutching the straw bag to her chest. *True blue*, she thought for courage, and plunged into her explanation.

"Even though my name *is* Angelique Dubonnet, everyone back home has always called me Angie. I'm not...who I said I was. I'm a small-town girl, living a small-town life, and this cruise is the most exciting thing I've done in my life." She'd crushed the lacy edges of the paper valentine in her fist. "I made up all that stuff about Angelique. For...excitement, I suppose. Because I'd saved for this vacation for years and I wanted it to be the cruise of a lifetime." She quailed inside. How could she have known that her lies would also lead to what might have been the love of a lifetime if only she'd given it an honest chance?

Niko said nothing. He stared at her, his hands in his pockets, his eyes still just as dark, but now mysterious as well. Perhaps he was withdrawing because he already knew she'd reneged on her promise of a no-strings-attached shipboard fling. Falling in love with your fling was the most binding string of them all, and she was tangled in it like a fish in a net.

She made herself go on. "I'm a nursery school teacher. I worked part-time at a convenience store to save extra money for this trip." She laughed dryly. "And that's where I became intimately acquainted with Daddy's Girls snack foods. I know their whole line backward and forward, but that's not the kind of thing you admit when you're trying to impress a Greek millionaire."

Niko turned his face aside, his expression tightening as if he was holding back a smile. Was he *amused* by her? She couldn't stand that. Even anger—or blunt dismissal—would be better than amusement!

She continued fiercely. "I was with you under false pretenses. Back home in Maple Hills, Michigan, I have a two-bedroom cottage that's mortgaged to the hilt. My roof leaks, the furnace-oil bill would choke a horse and for fun I shovel snow—not scale the Alps. I have two cats and lots of friends, but no fabulous, famous, world-renowned lovers." She took a deep breath. "Except, of course, for you." *And I don't have you any longer.* Deliberately, she let go of his valentine, symbolically cutting him loose. It wouldn't be as easy in her own case, but she'd have to do her best not to let him see that.

"World renowned?" he said with a provocative lift of one brow.

Angie blinked. He was so cool and self-possessed that she, in her fumbling, sweaty panic, couldn't bear it. The tight clench of her emotions started to loosen in sync with her muscles. Her eyes welled; her straw bag slithered from her grasp and plopped onto the rough wooden wharf. She grabbed it up, using the motion to dash at her embarrassing tears.

"Don't worry, though!" Her voice was watery, high-pitched. "A fling promised is a fling flung! I know this is goodbye!"

"Goodbye…" Niko echoed faintly, frowning.

Desperately Angie scrambled for the safety of the taxi-cab. She didn't want to hear any of the platitudes he might be compelled to speak for the sake of proper etiquette. If there was a proper etiquette when saying *sayonara* to a woman who'd done the things that she'd done the past night!

"Go," Angie said to the driver when Niko made no move to stop her. "Please go." She sniffled. "To the airport, as fast as you can."

The driver stepped on the gas hard enough to make the tires squeal. Which still didn't drown out the sound of Niko calling her name. "Angie!"

For an instant she believed that she might yet get a fairytale ending, but when she turned to look out the back window Nikolas wasn't chasing her cab, driven so wild with his sudden longing to hold her that he couldn't let her leave. He was only standing there, his hands in his pockets, the sunshine glancing off his blue-black hair. He didn't even wave until he saw her looking.

Angie faced forward. *That's that*, she thought bleakly. *It's over.*

One day she might remember her Valentine voyage fondly—perhaps when she was a little old lady in a rocking chair reminiscing about her life—but for now she could only close her eyes and swallow down her tears.

NIKOLAS DORIAN STOOD on the wharf and watched as Angie's cab disappeared into the traffic.

He was a bit stunned at the abruptness of her departure, but he certainly wasn't as shocked by her urgent

confession as she'd assumed. The details she'd spewed so
defiantly were about what he'd expected. He just hadn't
expected that she would be so hell-bent-for-leather in her
escape that he wouldn't have the chance to make his own
explanations.

He smiled. Angie might not be a globe-trotting adven-
turer, but she carried a strain of bold recklessness nonetheless. And, he mused, thinking of her daring lingerie
and the way her eyes had glittered as she'd placed her
foot on his shoulder, an equally strong carnal instinct.
Traits that just so happened to be wrapped in the kind of
cuddly body and sweetheart personality a guy could fall
in love with.

Nikolas chuckled. Miss Angelique Dubonnet had one
helluva shock coming her way.

Vicki Neill stepped up beside him. "Was that Angelique?" she said, waving after the cab.

"You might say that."

"I'm surprised you let her go so easily," Vicki scolded.

"Who says that I have?"

"Aha!" She beamed, pleased with her matchmaking
prowess. "So you're not adhering to the Greek millionaire
playboy theory of shipboard flings, Niko?"

Nikolas shrugged. "As I'm not a Greek millionaire
playboy…"

Vicki gaped at him. "You're not?"

He made part of the confession he'd intended to offer
Angie. "I'm a real-estate salesman from Detroit. I was
given this cruise as a reward for being the top money-
earner in my firm, but I'm nowhere close to millionaire
status. There might be some Greek blood in my family, a
few generations back."

"Then I suppose none of the other rumors are true,"
Vicki said, disappointed. "You're not a smuggler? An undercover cop?"

"Nope."

"Not even a real-estate swindler?"

"I sell tracts of rural real estate throughout the Midwest—all quite legally, I'm afraid."

Vicki sighed and swept off her straw hat. "No wonder Angelique got out of here so fast. What a letdown."

Nikolas only chuckled.

Vicki's eyeballs swiveled in horror. "Don't tell me! Not Angelique, too!" She jammed the hat back on her head. "No, no, please don't tell me. I don't want to know. Let her live on in my memory until it fades—an inspiration to me in my old age."

Nikolas nodded. "Oh, yes, she's an inspiration, all right."

Vicki peeked past her brim. "You rascal." She made shooing motions at him. "Well, go on, then. What are you waiting for? Catch up with her!"

"I believe that's just what I'll do." Nikolas exchanged warm goodbyes with Vicki and then strolled along the wharf toward his luggage. Even if he and Angie weren't on the same flight back to Michigan, he was bound to meet up with her sooner or later. It wouldn't take much to swing a deal that would send him north to her hometown. He might not wait even that long, though…seeing as how he wouldn't want to give her time to throw away that sexy black lingerie.

Oh, yes, Angie was in for it. Because if there was one thing he knew for sure about the past week it was that their affair was never meant to be short. In fact, their erotic valentine voyage had only just begun.…

If you enjoyed what you just read,
then we've got an offer you can't resist!

Take 2 bestselling love stories FREE!

Plus get a FREE surprise gift!

Clip this page and mail it to Harlequin Reader Service®

IN U.S.A.	IN CANADA
3010 Walden Ave.	P.O. Box 609
P.O. Box 1867	Fort Erie, Ontario
Buffalo, N.Y. 14240-1867	L2A 5X3

YES! Please send me 2 free Harlequin Temptation® novels and my free surprise gift. Then send me 4 brand-new novels every month, which I will receive months before they're available in stores. In the U.S.A., bill me at the bargain price of $3.12 plus 25¢ delivery per book and applicable sales tax, if any*. In Canada, bill me at the bargain price of $3.57 plus 25¢ delivery per book and applicable taxes**. That's the complete price and a savings of over 10% off the cover prices—what a great deal! I understand that accepting the 2 free books and gift places me under no obligation ever to buy any books. I can always return a shipment and cancel at any time. Even if I never buy another book from Harlequin, the 2 free books and gift are mine to keep forever. So why not take us up on our invitation. You'll be glad you did!

142 HEN CNEV
342 HEN CNEW

Name	(PLEASE PRINT)	
Address	Apt.#	
City	State/Prov.	Zip/Postal Code

* Terms and prices subject to change without notice. Sales tax applicable in N.Y.
** Canadian residents will be charged applicable provincial taxes and GST.
   All orders subject to approval. Offer limited to one per household.
   ® are registered trademarks of Harlequin Enterprises Limited.

TEMP99   ©1998 Harlequin Enterprises Limited

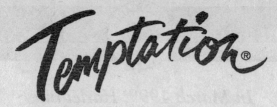

COMING NEXT MONTH

#721 SINGLE, SEXY...AND SOLD! Vicki Lewis Thompson
Bachelor Auction

When firefighter Jonah Hayes rescued a puppy, he had no idea
he'd become a hero. Or that he'd end up on the auction block.
But when Natalie LeBlanc, the puppy's sexy owner, bid $33,000
for him, Jonah's desire to test the chemistry between them
went up in smoke. Not only was Natalie out of his league...
she was out of her mind!

#722 UNLIKELY HERO Sandy Steen

Loner Logan Walker wasn't the type to rescue damsels in
distress. But even *he* couldn't leave gorgeous Paige Davenport
stranded by the side of the road. He told himself it was only
for a short time—but Paige managed to worm her way into his
life...and his heart. Little did he know that Paige had already
left one groom at the altar....

#723 IN THE DARK Pamela Burford
The Wrong Bed

Cat Seabright was expecting a friend who'd agreed to a "baby-
making date." All Brody Mikhailov expected was a warm bed
in New York City. And though a blackout threw everything
into confusion, both of them got what they were looking
for...in the dark.

#724 PRIVATE LESSONS Julie Elizabeth Leto
Blaze

Banker Grant Riordan was a bit of a stuffed shirt—until
"Harley" showed up and sent him reeling. The woman dressed
like an exotic dancer, had the eyes of an innocent...and didn't
know who she was! Grant considered her his every fantasy...
in the flesh. And while Harley searched for answers, Grant
learned some very *memorable* lessons....